Sparks fly from the moment Lori and Greg meet...

"Miss Wilson?" the tall man asked.

"Yes." Lori looked into eyes as blue and as cold as the glaciers she'd seen from the plane.

"I'm Greg Jensen. Plane's waiting. We'll get your luggage and be off." He looked from Joe to her, and his face was stiff.

"I...I don't have luggage. It got lost." Lori stammered. *What did I do to make him angry?* Mr. Jensen continued to stare at her with hard, cold eyes.

"Too bad about your luggage. I'll tell Hal to pick it up and bring it out with the mail when it finally gets here." He looked her up and down, taking in her skirt and high heels. Lori felt like a child caught with a dirty face. "Guess you'll have to fly in that outfit. Are you warm enough?"

"I'll be fine." Anger warmed her body in the chill wind. *Who does he think he is?* she fumed silently.

MARILOU H. FLINKMAN can't stay out of prison. She is highly active in prison ministry in her home state of Washington. This grandmother of nine also teaches beginning writing to college students while she adds to her own list of well over one hundred published short stories and articles. *The Alaskan Way* is her first inspirational romance.

The Alaskan Way

Marilou H. Flinkman

Heartsong Presents

To Mel, whose faith and encouragement
keep me writing

A note from the author:
I love to hear from my readers! You may write to me at
the following address: **Marilou H. Flinkman**
Author Relations
P.O. Box 719
Uhrichsville, OH 44683

ISBN 1-57748-270-0

THE ALASKAN WAY

Cover illustration by Brian Bowman.

one

Lori pressed her nose to the window of the 737 and watched the panorama below her with awe. Civilization had disappeared to be replaced by hundreds of tree-covered islands.

Unwanted tears burned her eyes as she thought of her brother's good-bye hug. Life had been so good, she mused, until Bob fell in love with Priscilla. He'd been more than a big brother, he was all the family she had. But now his life revolved around his wife. Well, at least Lori was free now, free of Priscilla's unwanted interference in her life.

Thoughts of Priscilla chased away the tears. *What does he see in her?* Lori asked herself for the hundredth time. She knew her big brother loved his wife, but in Lori's book, the woman couldn't do anything right. For instance, when the temperature in upstate New York soared to ninety degrees, Priscilla presented her sister-in-law with a down jacket to take to Alaska. "I guess I should thank the Lord she didn't bring me a dogsled," Lori muttered.

Get a hold of yourself, her mind scolded. *I know,* she answered herself, *I should be thankful Bob is happy.*

I'm on my own but I'm not alone, she thought. *I'm in Your hands, Lord. If You have something for me to do, I'm ready.*

She smiled when she remembered her friend Fred's reaction to her plans. "You're going to be a missionary?" he'd exclaimed.

"You make that sound like a disease, Fred."

"Cindy put you up to this, didn't she?"

"As a matter of fact, Cindy did help me find this job. Ever since her husband was stationed in Anchorage, I've been getting letters from her all about how wonderful Alaska is. So I asked her to look around for something I could do up there. I'm going to teach in a one-room school. And although I'm not officially a missionary, I'm looking at this as an opportunity to serve the Lord."

"Cindy always was a fool."

Lori felt her face get hot now as she remembered her anger. "Cindy's my best friend," she'd yelled at Fred.

Later Fred had apologized, but he'd begged Lori to keep her job teaching at the local school. Lori had already prayed long and hard, though, before she made the decision to accept the job in Alaska. She knew it meant giving up the security of having her brother to run to. It also meant leaving Fred—not that her feelings for him amounted to anything special, but she could count on good old Fred to take her out to dinner on Saturday night and to church on Sunday.

Lori sighed and settled back in her seat. Despite her excitement, she soon fell asleep.

The descending plane woke her. When she opened her eyes, the sight out the window set her heart pounding. Wisps of clouds brushed the glass, only partially blocking the view of rugged mountains. The snow-covered peaks looked close enough to touch. Then clouds thick as cotton obscured everything.

Lori didn't realize she'd been holding her breath until the plane dropped out of the clouds onto the runway, and she started to breathe again. "Thanks, Lord," she whispered as she gathered her belongings and prepared to exit. "I was afraid we might not make that landing."

Cindy wrapped Lori in a hug as soon as she stepped into the terminal. "Why ever did you carry your winter coat?" She took the down jacket and overnight case from Lori.

"Priscilla again," Lori moaned. "I guess she believes all Alaska is made up of ice, snow, and Eskimos. She gave me this jacket as a going-away gift." Lori looked around. "Where's Dan?"

"Air Force stuff. He's out on maneuvers. We'll be by ourselves, so we can have a chance to catch up on everything."

"I can't stay," Lori grumbled.

"Can't stay! Why not?"

"This Greg Jensen I'm supposed to meet sent a letter telling me to be in Kodiak on August first. His letter took two weeks to get to me. I'm sorry. When I talked to you on the phone, I didn't think I had to meet him until the tenth."

"That means you have to leave tomorrow," Cindy wailed. "Do you have reservations?"

Lori nodded. "Noon tomorrow."

"You're on the drunk tank."

"I'm what?"

Cindy sighed. "Guys come in from the brush to take in some city life—and they sober up on the plane back."

Lori tried to swallow the fear rising in her throat. "Are they really drunk?"

Cindy gave her a hug. "Loggers can be a rough lot. Their work is hard and dangerous and, yes, some of them come into town to get drunk."

"Can I go home now?" Lori asked plaintively.

Cindy laughed. "You've got a lot to learn about this country, but I know you're going to love it."

"Drunks and all?"

"Relax, there's no alcohol allowed in the logging camps, so you won't have any problems there."

Lori sighed and looked where the baggage had been brought in. "I don't see my suitcases and there aren't any more coming in."

"Let's go check on it."

"Maybe it got lost."

The ticket agent confirmed her fears. "Shouldn't take more than a day or two till we find your things, Miss Wilson."

"A day or two! What will I do?" she asked Cindy.

"I'll loan you something of mine," Cindy offered.

Lori looked up at Cindy and pictured her own five-foot-two-inch body in any of her friend's clothes. She started to giggle. "I don't think so." The giggle died in a strangled cry. "What will I wear tomorrow?"

Cindy put her arm around her and picked up the one bag Lori had. "Come on, we'll buy you a pair of kamiks and you can wear them with Priscilla's parka."

"Kamiks?"

"Leg warmers with feet. Natives make them out of skins."

"Cindy! It must be eighty degrees and you want to wrap me in furs and a parka?"

"Welcome to Alaska—and it's only seventy degrees." Cindy smiled. "We'll wash out your blouse tonight and it'll be dry by morning, good as new. The men will probably look you over—they're not used to seeing women in anything but jeans and flannel shirts—but you'll survive. And why don't I mail this parka to you? That way you don't have to lug it around all day tomorrow."

❧

With many hugs and promises to write often, the following day Lori left Cindy at the gate and boarded another airplane. This time she entered from the rear of the plane. The front seats had been removed and boxes of freight were piled in their place.

Nervously, she looked at the two men sprawled in the seats across from her. Long legs clad in faded jeans stretched into the aisle. Lori couldn't see their faces under the hats pulled over their eyes, but remembering that Cindy had called this flight the drunk tank sent a shiver down her spine. Were they really sleeping off a binge?

The plane took off, drawing her attention to the scene out the window. The mountains sparkled in snow coats, and she watched in awe as vast expanses of lakes, uninhabited land, and mountains spread out below her. Oh Lord, how beautiful is Your world.

"Is this your first trip to Kodiak?" A young man slipped into the seat next to her.

Lori sighed inwardly. "Does it show?"

"I'm Joe Nesbitt." The good-looking redhead offered her his hand. "I'm with the Coast Guard."

Lori twisted in the seat to shake the proffered hand. "Coast Guard in the air?"

Her seat mate laughed. "I've been on leave. What brings

you to Kodiak? Got a boyfriend stationed here?"

"I'm going to teach on Monk's Island."

"Too bad you won't be in town. I'd invite you to our church. We've got a great bunch of people." He talked about Kodiak and his work there and about his friends at church. The time passed quickly.

"When I get to town I'd like to meet your friends." Lori glanced out the window. "Oh, look at all the boats."

The plane circled over the marina and Lori held her breath as it appeared they would land in the water. "Sometimes the landing here can be rough, so don't be frightened," Joe warned. Suddenly, the plane dropped and she gripped the armrest as they hit the runway with a jolt. She was pushed against the back of the seat as the brakes were applied, and she caught herself bracing her feet as if to help hold the plane back as the mountains loomed at the end of the runway.

The loggers noticed her fear. One of them made a coarse joke, and the rest of them guffawed. Lori felt her face burn.

"One of the pilot's white-knuckle approaches. Scares you the first time." Joe's voice soothed her. "They have to hit the runway by a certain point to be extra safe. No problem, but nerve wracking when he drops on point."

Her dry throat didn't allow words, but she managed to smile.

"Can I help you with luggage?" he offered, stepping into the aisle.

"Thanks, my suitcases got lost."

"Do you have someone to meet you? My car is at the base right over there." He pointed to the low buildings near the runway.

Lori welcomed his friendly manner. "A Greg Jensen is supposed to meet me." Following Joe, she climbed down the steps of the plane as gracefully as she could. She watched the metal steps, held on to her carry-on bag, and wondered if the wind would tear her long hair loose from its barrette.

"Hey, there's a guy with your name on a sign."

Lori looked up, expecting to see a replica of the rough

men on the plane. Instead, a blond giant held a cardboard sign. He wore jeans and a plaid shirt, but he didn't have a brush cut and his face was not as weatherbeaten as the other lumbermen's. *Wonder if he chews tobacco?* Absently, Lori heard Joe ask when he would see her again.

"I don't know my phone number."

Joe laughed. "No phone on Monk's, Lori." He scribbled a number on a scrap of paper. "Call me when you get into Kodiak."

"Miss Wilson?" the tall man asked.

"Yes." Lori looked into eyes as blue and as cold as the glaciers she'd seen from the plane.

"I'm Greg Jensen. Plane's waiting. We'll get your luggage and be off." He looked from Joe to her, and his face was stiff.

"I. . .I don't have luggage. It got lost," Lori stammered. *What did I do to make him angry?* Mr. Jensen continued to stare at her with hard, cold eyes.

"Too bad about your luggage. I'll tell Hal to pick it up and bring it out with the mail when it finally gets here." He looked her up and down, taking in her skirt and high heels. Lori felt like a child caught with a dirty face. "Guess you'll have to fly in that outfit. Are you warm enough?"

"I'll be fine." Anger warmed her body in the chill wind. *Who does he think he is?* she fumed silently.

"Well, come along then." Jensen turned and walked away.

No way will I let this brute know he upsets me, Lori thought as she struggled to keep up with his long stride. The high heels handicapped her as she tried to hold her hair up and her skirt down in the breeze. She followed him across the blacktop to a small blue and white plane. "Oh no," she groaned, seeing the two loggers from the Anchorage flight standing next to the plane.

"Where's your stuff?" Jensen growled at them.

"Hal checked us out, Chief."

Lori saw the blond giant look at the pilot. "They're clean, Greg," he called as he swung down to the ground. "Where's the lady's bags?"

"Yah, Chief, she could have hooch in that little bag of hers."

"Dry up, George, and get on board." Greg turned to Lori. "We don't allow alcohol on the island." He handed her carry-on bag to Hall.

Lori stood in silence, looking from one man to another. Hal held her bag and asked, "You want to ride shotgun, miss?"

"Shotgun?"

Hal grinned. "Just you climb up there by me. Buckle yourself into the copilot's seat."

"She's too short to see over the dash, Hal," one of the loggers protested.

"She can see out the side, you drunken cowboy," Hal told George as he climbed into the plane. "You ready, Greg?"

Mr. Jensen stood by the hangar talking to people inside. "Sooner the better," he yelled back.

Hal took Lori's elbow. "Let me help you up, miss."

She noted with relief that with his body he shielded her assent into the small plane, while he tactfully kept his eyes on her face. "I lost my luggage and only had this outfit to wear," she explained as he helped her climb to the front of the plane.

"My pleasure. Don't get to see a lady dressed up very often around here."

The two loggers and Greg Jensen settled in and Hal revved the motor. The small plane soon climbed into the vast blue sky, and Lori caught her breath at the panorama below. Islands of trees, bays, and infinite beauty spread out before her.

"That's You-sink-ee."

Lori nodded, not knowing what she was supposed to be looking at. The roar of the engines made small talk impossible. Hal kept the plane low and occasional currents over the land masses bounced them up and down.

This stimulating enough for you? her mind asked.

Beats riding the Ferris wheel with Fred, her thoughts answered.

Hal circled the plane down and Lori gasped as he deftly flew between two cliffs. She was afraid the wings would touch the land. He circled again and landed the plane on a bay, taxiing onto the beach.

Excitement tingled through Lori. "That was great! I've never been in a floatplane before."

"Only way to get around in this country."

The men in the back were getting out, and Lori heard shouts of greeting. As carefully as her high heels and skirt would allow, she crawled ungracefully out of the plane, gritting her teeth in embarrassment. As she stepped onto the ground, her heels wobbled. She stumbled forward, twisting her ankle.

A grizzled old man with a shaggy mane and beard of black and gray offered her a hand. "This the new schoolmarm?" He guided her to a battered pickup truck standing by the plane. "I'll run her up to her place and be back for the groceries."

Lori looked up to the glacial stare of Greg Jensen. "I wouldn't want to take your men away from their work. If you'll point the way, I'll walk." She hoped her words were as cold as his manner.

"It's not my time he's wasting. Go ahead, Jim, before we have to fly her out with a broken leg."

Lori seethed under his words.

"Don't pay him no mind, miss. He don't know how to smile."

"Thanks, Jim. I'm Lori Wilson." As she climbed into the truck, she explained again about her lost luggage and apologized for the way she was dressed.

"You look real pert, Miss Lori." He patted Lori's hand on the seat next to him and chuckled. "You know, the last teacher showed up in July wearing a ski parka and boots." His eyes twinkled. "Think she expected to find Eskimos in igloos."

Lori closed her eyes and said a quick prayer for Cindy's good sense in offering to mail the down jacket. She opened her eyes as the truck jolted to a stop beside a mobile home.

"Here's home. You got groceries on the plane?"

"I only flew in from Anchorage this morning. Can't I buy stuff here?"

Jim chuckled again. "If you chew tobacky or drink soda

pop, you can get it at the company office."

Lori felt the panic start to rise.

"Here." Jim pulled a pink form out of his pocket. "You check off what you want and I'll be sure Hal brings it on the next flight."

"When will that be?"

"Depends on the weather. Should be tomorrow, but could be next week."

"Oh." Lori fought down the panic.

"Don't worry. You can get some grub at the bunkhouse. Got to get back now. I'll pick up the grocery list shortly." He started the truck and as he turned around to leave, he stuck his head out the window. "Some stuff come for you on the barge last week. I piled it in the wanagan."

"Wanagan? I don't even speak the language," she muttered, waving good-bye to Jim. "Well, Lord, I got this far. Now what?"

She walked up the steps and entered an enclosed wooden porch, which had been built on the side of the mobile home. There sat her boxes. "Well, now I know wanagan is another name for an enclosed porch."

She kicked off her shoes and started her inspection tour, thinking about the people she'd met. Rough loggers, icy Mr. Jensen. She shuddered. At least Joe Nesbitt in Kodiak and Jim in camp were friendly. . .and Hal, the pilot.

Lori walked through the kitchen to the living room. Her feet sunk gratefully into the soft carpet as she walked to the window. She looked out over the rippling blue water to the mountains on the other side. These were the soft rounded mountains she was used to seeing in upstate New York, and suddenly she felt less lonely. "It's beautiful," she whispered.

Further inspection showed that her mobile home sat on a bluff, one in a row of a half dozen. She looked down the rocky road to a large metal shed where several heavy equipment rigs were being worked on. Another hill rose on the other side of the shops where more mobile homes sat. She spotted a small red building she thought must be the schoolhouse. Hal's blue and white widgeon sat on the rocky beach with Jim's old pickup nearby.

"I'm going to like it. I know I'm going to like it," Lori told herself.

Turning back to look over her home, she admired the davenport and chair. An open bookcase separated the living room and kitchen. Bright yellow curtains framed the kitchen window over a table and chairs. She wandered down the hall to find two bedrooms with a bathroom between. Spotting the built-in desk and bookshelves in the smaller bedroom, she thought of the boxes of books and household things waiting to be unpacked. Hurrying back to the wanagan, she started pulling open cartons to find the things that would make this her own home.

two

Lori had packed her dishes between layers of clothes, towels, and bedding. Hastily, she unfolded a pair of jeans and a pink sweater and stacked the plates they were protecting on the floor. By the time Jim knocked on the door, her skirt and blouse lay in a heap on the bedroom floor, and Lori wore jeans and a sweater. Her long hair hung loose to her waist.

"Come in, Jim. I'm almost finished with the list."

He set her carry-on bag down in the wanagan. "You ain't no bigger than a minute."

Lori felt herself blush as she looked down at her bare feet. "Uh, come on in. The list's in the kitchen."

She heard him shuffle along behind her. "I found some things in the cupboard. Do they belong to someone?"

He shook his head. "Most folks who move out do that. Helps the next one comin' along." He took the pink form she offered him. "Weather looks good, so Hal should be in tomorrow. Usually the lists get mailed to the store. They box the stuff up and deliver it to the airport. Suppose to be in Thursday or Friday if it ain't too windy or foggy."

Lori opened her billfold. "I don't have any idea what I owe."

He waved her money back. "Store will send you a bill once a month. Easier for everybody that way. Got to run now. Hal's waitin'. He don't usually wait no more than for me to unload the freight."

"I've been a lot of bother," she said as she followed him to the door, "but I'll learn as fast as I can."

"Bunkhouse is the long white building. Office's next door. I'm usually around one or t'other if you need anything."

"Thanks, Jim. I appreciate it."

Lori turned back to the boxes. The sun felt good streaming in the door, so she left it open. Engrossed in the unpacking,

Lori didn't hear anyone come up the steps. She jumped when a small voice broke the silence.

"Mama says you're to come to supper."

Lori looked from the box she knelt by into the brownest eyes she'd ever seen. The little girl looked down and shyly twisted the edge of her sweater. "What's your name?" Lori asked in a quiet voice.

The brown eyes looked up, watching, as wary as a frightened deer. "Peggy."

"Do you go to school, Peggy?"

"We do lessons with Mama and mail them to the teacher."

"Haven't you ever been to school?"

"To the movies." The little voice gained strength. The eyes were no longer timid.

"You have movies in the schoolhouse?" Lori stayed on her knees, curious about the pretty child on her doorstep.

"Every Saturday night. It's Mama's turn to make popcorn." The heart-shaped face framed in dark bouncing curls looked at her. "Want to come?"

Lori reached out to touch the springy curls. "I'd love to."

"Now you have to come for supper. Mama said it's almost ready and I should show you the way."

Lori stood up thinking, *Shoes, I don't have any shoes.* "Just a minute, Peggy. I have to find some sneakers."

"Not nice to sneak."

"Huh?" Lori looked up from digging in a box. *Language again,* she thought, holding up a pair of tennis shoes. "I meant shoes."

"Oh."

Lori pulled on the tennies and reached for the little girl's hand.

"We live on the other hill," Peggy explained.

"Do we go by the school?"

"Want to see it?"

"If it won't make your mother wonder where you are."

"She knows I wouldn't go out of camp. The bears would get me."

What a horrible story to frighten a child with, Lori thought, as they walked by the machine shed. Several men waved and Peggy waved back. "My daddy drives a big cat out in the woods," the child chirped.

Following in silence, Lori regretted leaving her hair loose. The breeze blew long strands around her face, but she forgot her discomfort as they went up the steps of the red building. Sun streamed in the windows, showing the bare room. Desks were piled along one side and folding chairs sat in rows facing a portable movie screen. Lori moved around the room, deciding how to arrange her schoolroom.

"What are you kids doing in here?" a deep voice demanded.

Peggy stood by the door, and Lori turned in time to see the child's fright as Greg pushed past the girl into the room. Anger flooded through her.

"Leave that child alone!" she snapped. "This is my schoolroom and no one, not even you, will rough up my students." Through the red haze of fury she saw Greg's look of amazement. It didn't slow her down a bit. Reaching out, she put a protective hand on Peggy's shoulder.

"I. . .I'm sorry, Miss Wilson. I thought you were a kid fooling around in here."

"Well, I'm not." Her anger still burned.

"Are you comfortable? Have you found the things you need?" He stood like an errant child.

"Yes, thank you," Lori snapped. "Now if you'll get out of our way, Peggy and I are going to supper." She set her jaw, tilted her chin up, and stormed past Greg with Peggy in tow. "That man makes it hard to be a Christian," she muttered.

Once back on the path, Peggy pointed to the third mobile home on the right. "I live there."

Lori swallowed her anger. "Are you all right? Did Mr. Jensen push you hard?"

"I'm okay. He just startled me." The child bounded up the steps and banged open the door of the wanagan. Two more children, younger than Peggy, peeked around the door as Lori went up the steps.

"Mark, Aaron, get out of the way. Let the lady in." A young woman holding a baby on her hip greeted Lori. "Welcome. I was beginning to think Peggy couldn't find you."

"She's been a great guide."

"Come in. I'm Theresa O'Brien."

"Hi, I'm Lori Wilson." Peggy kicked her shoes off and Lori noticed the row of boots and shoes by the door.

Theresa must have seen her puzzled look. "I'll loan you some slippers. So much volcanic ash around here, the only way to keep a clean house is to not wear shoes."

"You have a volcano?" Lori shuddered.

"Not to worry. Katmai blew up in 1912, but the dust lingers on."

Lori slipped off her shoes and followed Theresa and the children. "I sure appreciate your invitation. My cupboards are pretty bare and you don't have a corner store."

"Didn't anyone warn you about that?" Theresa put the baby in a high chair and handed Lori a pair of slipper-socks from a nearby basket of laundry.

Looking around, Lori realized this mobile home was laid out like her own. "You have four children?" she asked, wondering how the young mother managed to fit them in the small space.

Theresa stood only a couple inches taller than Lori, but bearing children had spread her figure a little more. She smiled happily at the question. "All ours. Peggy is seven, Mark five, Aaron three, and. . ." She stooped to pick up a toy and put it back on the high chair. "Katie's nine months." She followed Lori's look and laughed. "It's tight quarters, but we have a triple-decker bunk bed and a crib in the biggest bedroom. Dennis and I have the smaller one." She waved at the toys spread over the living room. "Kids never have had a lot of room to play so they don't mind it."

"You're thoughtful to ask me for supper."

"My pleasure. News from the outside! I'll bend your ears with questions." She poured two mugs of coffee and sat at the kitchen table with Lori. Peggy hugged her mother's side.

"Mama, Teacher yelled at Greg when he told me to get out of the school."

"What were you doing in the school?"

The child's eyes were big and her face shone with innocence. "Just showing it to Teacher."

"I did fly off the handle," Lori admitted. "He thought I was a kid, too, and it made me mad."

Theresa laughed and hugged her daughter. Mark and Aaron stopped building their block city and looked at the women. "Good for you. Don't let him scare you. He's really soft as butter inside, but to him showing emotion is a venial sin."

The door opened and the boys raced down the hall to the wanagan, yelling, "Daddy, Daddy."

A broad-shouldered man with black curly hair, wearing dirty jeans and a plaid shirt, strode into the kitchen in his stocking feet. He held a boy under each of his muscular arms.

Peggy tugged at his pant leg, demanding attention. "We got company."

Lori saw Theresa look at her husband with warm affection. "Den, this is Lori, the new schoolteacher."

He swung his sons to the floor and buried Lori's small hand in his large, work-hardened one. "Welcome to Monk's, Lori." He turned to his wife. "I'm starved. When do we eat?"

Theresa jumped up. "All ready." She gave him a quick kiss as she told the kids to wash up. Katie started banging a spoon on her high chair tray. "Daddy's little darling is demanding equal time."

Dennis picked the baby up and held her high so she touched the ceiling. She gurgled and crowed in delight.

The supper of baked salmon tasted delicious. "I've never had salmon like that before," Lori said.

"You'll learn to hate it like the rest of us. The diet around here is venison, salmon, halibut, and whatever else we find on the beach. You'll know you belong here when you start dreaming of a thick, fat beefsteak."

Theresa busied herself clearing off the table. She refused to let Lori help. "Too small for more than one cook in this kitchen." Lori marveled at how the young mother cooked meals and fed a big family in such a small area.

"You got in today?" Dennis asked.

"I think I left home yesterday, spent last night in Anchorage with a friend, and arrived here this afternoon. With jet lag, I'm not too sure on time or day yet."

"We'll let you have a couple days, then we'll give you the fifty-cent tour of the island."

"I have a lot to learn. The information I got with the job description left out a lot of details."

Theresa refilled the coffee cups. "Nobody told her about ordering food."

"Jim gave me an order slip today and I hope I'll get stuff tomorrow. He said I could eat at the bunkhouse." Lori grimaced. "That didn't sound too appealing."

"You met George and Shorty already, huh?" Dennis laughed.

"They were on the plane from Anchorage."

"Yeah, Whitney's been cussing those two for a week." Dennis shook his head. "Sad what liquor can do. George is an excellent engineer, but every so often the booze gets the better of him. Used to go into Kodiak, but Whitney would search him out, sober him up, and get him back on the job. This time he went to Anchorage. Greg had to meet you, and I heard he escorted George back. Shorty's George's silent partner. Likes to get boozed up, but he's still a company man and lets Whitney know where they are. He must have been enjoying the fling this time 'cause he didn't radio the office till day before yesterday."

Theresa sat down with the baby in her arms. "Lori's not interested in camp politics."

"What else is there around here? You like to hunt and fish, Lori?"

She sipped her coffee, hoping it would wake her up. Jet lag, excitement, and travel were beginning to show. "I like to fish, but we never went hunting."

"Better give her some meat and fish, honey," he told his wife. Turning back to Lori, he asked, "They have a freezer in that place of yours?"

Lori thought of the big white chest in the wanagan. "Yes, I didn't look at it, but I guess that's what it is."

Baby Katie sucked greedily on a bottle. Her mom said, "You order everything in bulk around here. We can go for days in the winter when no plane can get in."

"I'm going to feel silly ordering a case of soup for just me."

"You'll be glad you've got it. You baked bread before?"

"No. I'm not much of a cook."

"We can do things together and share the results," Theresa offered.

"Dennis may not like that if he has to eat any of my cooking."

He put his cup down. "I'll try anything once." He tickled his tiny daughter. "Want me to get the kids to bed?"

Theresa's eyes shone. "So I can gossip with Lori?"

He kissed his wife's forehead. "You deserve it."

Theresa looked shyly at Lori while Dennis went into the living room, yelling in mock anger at the boys and Peggy. By the sounds of the giggles and squeals, the children were delighted with the game. "It's rough being isolated, but Dennis is so good, I try not to complain."

"How long have you been here?"

"I haven't been off the island in eight months." She cradled the now sleeping baby. "Katie was born in Kodiak. I stayed with friends till she was a month old."

Lori thought of being trapped in a two-bedroom trailer with four children day in and day out. "How do you stand it?"

She watched Theresa sigh. "Hard sometimes. I really miss my church." Theresa looked up. "There are twenty families here. Must be sixteen kids. We play lots of games, have pot-lucks at the schoolhouse. The company has a movie on Saturday night. They're 1940s vintage and kind of fun."

"Peggy told me about the movies. Said it was your turn to make popcorn. Could I help?"

"Oh, you'll get your turn. Mike's the bunkhouse cook. He'll give you the popcorn and butter, you supply the labor.

You have a popcorn maker?"

Lori thought of the one Priscilla had given her. At the time Lori had wondered what to do with it and had only packed it because she didn't want to hurt her sister-in-law's feelings. "Yes, I got one last Christmas."

The laughter and whoops died down in the other room. "I better put Katie in her crib."

"I should get home."

"Oh, please, not yet. It's so great to see a new face."

Dennis came back. "Come sit in an easy chair."

Lori followed him into the living room. He busied himself picking up toys and blocks. "Wish I could afford to send Theresa to town more often. She's a brick to put up with this place."

"Is it expensive?" Lori thought of the salary she expected to receive.

"The hundred-dollar plane fare is only the beginning. Meals, rooms, renting a car, everything costs twice what you'd pay down south. We used to be friends with a couple in the Coast Guard and could stay with them. He got transferred six months ago."

"Why do you stay?" Lori had the question out before she realized how rude it sounded.

Dennis didn't seem to notice. "The money. Pure and simple. If we stay here five years, we can buy a nice spread in Oregon. Have the kind of place we want to raise the kids and still live on what I can earn down there."

Theresa curled up on the davenport. "There are two kinds of people in Alaska. The ones who love it and the ones who want the big money. Guess we fall into the last category. It's expensive to raise a family, and this way we can do it the way we want. Came here when Aaron was six months old, so we're halfway to our dream."

Dennis took his wife's hand, "Why did you come, Lori? You seeking a fortune or adventure?"

"I think I'm running away from home."

"So why here? This isn't the end of the world, but you can

see it from here."

Lori smiled. "My best friend's husband is stationed at Elmendorf Airbase at Anchorage. She kept telling me about the wonderful country and sending me information about jobs. I wanted to try something different, and here I am."

"Do you have moments of insanity often?"

Lori and Theresa laughed.

"Or maybe you dreamed of romance and high adventure. If you thought you could romance the monks, they're long gone."

Theresa pulled her hand away. "Be good. You'll embarrass the poor girl."

Lori enjoyed the banter and asked, "Were there really monks here?"

"Sure. When Baranov settled Kodiak Island for the Russians, Father Herman brought the Russian Orthodox Church. There are still a few monks in Kodiak. Anyway, back then the monks had a retreat on this island. You can still see parts of the cabins on the other side of Goose Bay. The natives treat it as a holy place."

"Are there native Alaskans living on this island?"

"Not anymore. The last village got wiped out in the earthquake of 1964. Uzinkie is about the biggest village left and it's on Spruce Island."

"You-sink-ee? Hal pointed it out and I thought it sounded like quicksand."

Both Dennis and Theresa laughed. Through her giggles, Theresa said, "I hope you didn't tell Greg that."

"No. I rode up front with Hal and didn't talk to anyone else."

"Greg grew up in Uzinkie, according to the rumors around here," Dennis explained.

Theresa sighed. "Some of the women say the Norse god Thor left him there."

Dennis nodded. "I'd agree when he gets to thundering about the way Whitney logs."

"I'm so confused," Lori complained. "The state certified me to teach and Whitney Logging furnished my home.

Where does Greg fit? Isn't he the boss?"

Dennis sat up and threaded his fingers over his knees. "Greg works for K.A.T. That stands for Koniag, Aleut, and Tlingit Native Corporations. They own the land and Whitney has a contract to log off the trees. Greg is the forestry consultant hired to keep Whitney honest. Greg isn't a native, but you'd think he was the way he guards their rights. Good thing, really. Keeps us all honest."

"You aren't usually so kind. Going soft?" Theresa asked her husband.

"Oh, I get ticked off at Greg, but he's just doing his job. I've seen Whitney try to use cheaper materials on the roads, try to cut corners. Without Greg, the native corporations would get robbed blind. I guess it's his attitude that bothers me most. The guy is a cold fish."

"Handsome, though."

Lori watched Dennis poke his wife playfully. "You starting to look at other men, huh?"

She giggled. "Maybe Lori can thaw him out."

"Not me. I'd be happy if I never saw him again."

"He's a loner, so you won't see much of him."

"Right now, I can't keep my eyes open to see anything." Lori got up and stretched. "Your supper tasted great and the company has been perfect."

Dennis stood with his arm around Theresa as Lori pulled on her shoes. "Please come see me again," Theresa begged. "Aaron is hard to keep track of when I'm carrying Katie, so I don't go far."

"I will. Maybe you could introduce me to the other parents."

With a final wave, Lori started back to her mobile home. The western sky blazed with colors. Purple shadows crept up the eastern horizon, ready to coat the late night sky. The breeze had died down and the still water mirrored shades of yellow and gold. The air felt cool and Lori hugged her arms in front of her. *Got to send Priscilla a thank-you note for the jacket,* she thought. *By winter I might be glad I've got it.*

Instead of going in her home, Lori walked to the front of her trailer to look over the bay and the changing colors of the late evening sunset. A large fallen log rested at the edge of the bluff and made a perfect spot to sit and drink in the beauty around her. A huge orange striped cat jumped on the other end of the log.

"Did I steal your spot?"

The cat eyed Lori with a malevolent stare.

"Marmalade doesn't like women." Greg's deep voice surprised Lori. "I came to see if you needed anything, but you weren't home."

"Thank you, I've been to the O'Briens'." *I will be friendly,* Lori told herself.

"Good people. Theresa would be the one to think to feed you." He stood with one foot on the log and leaned forward on his knee, looking over the bay.

Lori followed his gaze. "And the heavens will declare the glory of God," she quoted.

Greg didn't answer. After a long silence, he said, "I never get tired of looking over this bay. It's always changing." His voice had a distant, almost reverent tone. The cat came over to rub against his leg and purr. He scratched the animal's head. "We can't have dogs here, but old Marmalade can fend for himself."

"Why no dogs?"

He sighed and sat on the log with his back to the bay. Still patting the cat, he said, "The brown bears here are mean. You never know what they'll do. Dog wouldn't stand a chance."

"Peggy mentioned bears today. I thought some grown-up had just scared her with bear stories to keep her from wandering off. Are they a real danger?"

"Don't leave camp. . .stay on the road. . .oh, and put any garbage in a plastic bag in your wanagan. Jim hauls the stuff out to be buried in different sites. Bears are a real danger all right."

"I feel like this place should come with a book of instructions."

"Takes awhile to get used to. Ever spent any time in back

country before?"

"Somehow I don't think a camp on Lake Ontario counts as back country."

He smiled, and the effect caused Lori to take a second look. *Maybe he's not so mean after all,* she thought.

Greg stood up and the cat started toward the trailer next to Lori's. "You like to fish?"

"Yes. The salmon I ate tonight was delicious. I'd like to try my luck, but I didn't bring a fishing pole."

He pointed to the boat next to the mobile home where the cat stood. "I've got a boat and lots of fishing gear. The silvers are running now. Want to try your luck?"

Old stone face trying to be nice! Lori stood up. Her head barely came to his shoulder, and she had to tilt her head back to look into his eyes. Were they blue-violet or did the sunset play games with her sight? "Sure, got to get my winter supplies in."

A look of surprise flashed quickly across his face. "I'll stop by when I get in from checking road tomorrow. If you're still willing, we'll go fishing."

Impulsively Lori offered, "If you tell me what time you'll be in, I'll have supper ready."

"Be early. We'll eat when we get back from fishing. You like shrimp?"

Lori envisioned a bowl of cracked ice with nice pink prawns and red cocktail sauce. "Love them."

"We'll pull my pots on the way in and cook some up fresh."

She vowed to run to Theresa first thing in the morning to ask how to cook shrimp. She put her hand out to Greg. "That's a deal."

Again the smile broke through his reserve, allowing his perfect features to soften from stone to splendid. He took her proffered hand in a firm grip. "Deal."

Slowly she walked back to her wanagan door. Marmalade sat on the steps of the home next door. *Hmmm, Greg and I must be neighbors.* She went in, flipped on a light, and remembered she still had to make her bed with the sheets and bear's paw quilt she'd unpacked earlier.

three

The next morning, Lori gasped when she looked at the time; she'd slept nearly twelve hours. She bounced out of bed and pulled open the heavy drapes. The sun shown in a crystal blue sky and treetops swayed gently in the breeze.

The sound of an approaching airplane sent her scurrying. "Groceries. . .Jim will be here and I'm not dressed. . .can't let him know I slept till eleven," she muttered to herself as she pawed through piles of folded clothes, looking for something to wear.

Fifteen minutes later, when Jim yelled "Hello" at the wanagan door, Lori had on jeans and a sweatshirt. She'd found time to wash her face, but her hair still hung loose down her back.

"Come in," she called.

"Got more to deliver. I'll just set your box down here. Don't look like you plan to eat much."

She felt herself blush as she stammered, "I, uh, filled out the list in a hurry. Probably missed a few things. I'll get them next week."

"You let me know if'n you need anything."

"Thanks, Jim."

Lori watched him get in his battered truck before she turned back to her house. Partly filled boxes and odd stacks of clothes, household items, and books were scattered everywhere. She found room on the table to put down the box of groceries and started opening cupboards.

Hunger pangs reminded her it had been a long time since Theresa's dinner. Lori put the tea kettle on the stove and carried a stack of bath towels to the linen closet while she waited for the water to boil.

With a sandwich in one hand and a mug of tea in the other,

Lori escaped her cluttered house to sit on the log overlooking the bay. Marmalade stalked out of his place in the sun, and Lori offered a bit of sandwich to her feline antagonist. He sniffed, then slowly, with a haughty twitch of his tail, went back to his sunny spot.

"So you don't like tuna fish either. What do you like?"

"You've only been here a day and already you're talking to yourself." Lori looked up to see Theresa with Katie in a baby backpack and Aaron in a harness attached to a rope. Peggy and Mark ran along behind.

Lori smiled. "Worse, I'm talking to a snooty cat." She motioned to where Marmalade had been sitting, but at the first sound of children, the cat had fled. "So far he doesn't like women, tuna fish, or kids."

"Try raw salmon."

"Hey, I'm going fishing. Greg's taking me out in his boat this afternoon."

Theresa snapped back in surprise. Katie didn't like the sudden motion; she grabbed the bar on her pack and howled.

Lori jumped up to try to soothe the baby's ruffled feelings. Katie howled louder. "Come in and let this abused child out of her cage." Lori scooped up the willing Aaron and started for the house. "The place is a mess. I can't believe I stuffed so much junk in a few boxes."

Theresa sat on the edge of the davenport and eased the backpack off her shoulders. She made a rueful face at her unhappy daughter. "Now you know why I don't go out a lot."

"I'm honored." Lori hugged the little boy and put him on the floor by his mother. "I don't have much to offer. Would the kids like some crackers?"

Theresa looked around. "They're like me. Only hungry to see something different." She put Katie on the floor next to Aaron. "We came to invite you to a potluck Friday night at the schoolhouse."

"Sounds great. What can I do to help?"

"Come over on Friday and help us set up. You'll meet the other mothers then. We'll have the potluck on Friday and a movie on Saturday. The excitement may be too much."

"Can't be that bad." Lori sat on the floor next to Katie and Aaron, who were busy crumbling crackers. Peggy and Mark could be heard outside throwing rocks over the bluff. Shaking her head in wonder, Lori told Theresa, "I don't know how you manage with all the kids."

"Aren't you a schoolteacher? I'd think a room full of twenty or thirty a lot more intimidating than only four."

"True, but I get them after they can take care of themselves. You know, potty trained, walking, talking. And remember, I only have them a few hours a day."

Theresa went to the window to check on her two oldest children. "I like it this way." She came back and sat down when Lori brought her a cup of tea. "Oh, I get tired and yell at them, but then they'll do something cute and make it all worthwhile."

"Tell me about the other parents. Have any of the kids ever gone to regular school?"

"Most have. We have quite a turnover around here—not everyone can take this life. By hiring a teacher, Whitney thought more families would stay." Theresa put her cup on the end table, stuck a plastic duck in front of Katie, and pulled a toy car from another pocket for Aaron.

"Do I detect a note of bitterness?"

Theresa smiled wanly. "Sometimes. Mostly I miss being able to go to church. We take turns doing Bible study, but it's not like sitting in a pew and listening to a sermon." She sipped her cup of tea. "But enough whining, tell me about the outside world. What's it like to walk up and down the aisles of a grocery store?"

Lori felt sheepish. "I don't know. I ate in the dorm in college and lived with my brother and his wife till I came here. Other than picking up bread or milk, I've stayed out of stores. I have bought clothes, of course," she added.

Theresa sighed and put her cup down. "You were in paradise and didn't even know it. Catalogues are all right, but it's not the same."

"Maybe I'll feel that way eventually. Up till now, shopping has been a bore." Lori got up to fetch the teapot. "Tell me more about this Jensen."

"You really going fishing with him?"

Lori turned in surprise. "Is there something wrong?" She grinned. "You think he plans to drown me?"

"He takes Dennis or some of the other guys out, but never a woman." Theresa looked at Lori in mock seriousness as she accepted the refilled cup. "Can you swim? Sure as heck that boat will sink with a woman in it."

"I can swim and I'm used to boats. I grew up on Lake Ontario, but I've never fished for salmon. Never caught more than perch or trout."

Theresa retrieved Aaron, who had found a stack of books. "Can't help you much there. With the kids to care for, I don't do much fishing. I spend all my time in a boat counting to make sure no one is overboard." She got the little ones interested in some old magazines Lori found in a cupboard. "You have any boots?"

"I brought some fancy fur boots to wear in the snow. What kind of boots do I need?"

"Alaskan tennis shoes."

Lori raised her eyebrows.

Theresa was serious. "What size do you wear?"

"Five."

"Uh-oh, mine'll be way too big. Maybe with some heavy socks they'll do. How soon are you leaving?"

Lori shrugged her shoulders. "Greg said he'd be by this afternoon after he checked roads. Oh, that's another problem. He said we'd cook shrimp when we got back and I don't know how."

Theresa knelt on the floor, brushing up cracker crumbs. "Walk back with me now and you can get my boots."

Lori helped get the squirming Katie secured in the backpack. "I'll watch Aaron," she said, waving the rope harness aside. "What's the big deal about boots? I can go barefoot or wear old tennis shoes."

"And freeze to death! They launch the boats right off the beach and you have to wade out to get in the boat."

Theresa called to Peggy and Mark, who were trying to coax Marmalade out of hiding. As they walked back down the road past the maintenance shed and up the other side to the O'Briens', Theresa explained. "Everyone has boots. They are something like what we used to call barn boots, only here they are knee high and reddish brown. You won't believe the mud around here."

When they reached Theresa's with all the children accounted for, Lori tried Theresa's boots and decided it was a good thing she wouldn't have to walk much. "I feel like I'll walk right out of them. Now tell me what to do with shrimp."

"He'll probably pull his shrimp pot on the way in. You'll have to head them within thirty minutes."

"Head them? In what direction?"

Theresa stopped midway to putting Katie down. "Direction?"

"You said to head the shrimp and I don't even know what direction."

Theresa dropped the startled Katie in her bed and collapsed in a chair.

Watching her new friend rock in laughter, Lori dared to ask, "Do I need a compass?"

Tears streamed down Theresa's face. "Stop, stop," she gasped, "I can't laugh anymore."

"Could you let me in on the joke?" Lori asked. "All I want to know is what to do with shrimp."

"Lori, you're too much." Theresa wiped her tears away still muttering, "What direction."

"Could we start over?"

Struggling to catch her breath and stop laughing, Theresa told her, "You pull the heads off the shrimp right away and the black streak, like a vein of ink, will peel right off."

Lori's stomach lurched, but she said nothing. She didn't want to start Theresa laughing again.

"Cooking them is easy. You just boil them in salted water six or eight minutes. Peel off the shell, dip them in melted garlic butter, and you've got yourself a feast."

Lori hadn't got past pulling their heads off. She thanked Theresa for the help, then glanced at her watch and yelped. "It's four o'clock. I better get home before Greg does."

Katie had fallen asleep, but Aaron planted a slobbery kiss on her cheek before she started back up the hill toward her home.

"Good luck. Catch a big one," Theresa called after her.

"Thanks." Lori waved, thinking, *Big fish, yes, but, Lord, please let the shrimp pot be empty.*

🙣

By hurrying, Lori had most of the things cleared off the kitchen chairs and her trailer beginning to look like a home by the time Greg knocked at her back door.

"Hi," she greeted him. She stood in heavy wool socks, a pair of jeans, and warm wool sweater; her hair hung in one neat plait down her back. She thought she read approval in his look.

"I'll go hook up the boat. Come over when you're ready and you can ride down to the beach with me," he told her.

Lori nodded. "I'll be right over." She looked at the boots Theresa had loaned her and decided for now to pull off the socks and wear a pair of tennis shoes. Stuffing the heavy socks into the boots, she grabbed them, a windbreaker, and a hat and headed out the door after Greg.

"You know how to launch a boat?" Greg asked.

"No," she admitted. "We always kept our boat at the dock."

"You have been out in a boat then."

His condescending manner made her blood boil. She tried to keep the anger out of her voice. "Why don't you use the dock here?"

"Oh, you mean that pier?" He pointed to the long cement structure jutting out into the bay. "That's built for the barge. Way too tall for a fishing boat."

He started the truck and they headed toward the water. "You do a lot of fishing?"

"Some." *I must be nuts going out with this guy. I'll show*

him I can fish as well as any man.

Conversation ceased as he backed the boat into the water. A couple of men Lori hadn't met offered to help. Greg backed farther into the water till the boat floated free of the trailer. He pulled the truck and trailer back on the beach. "You wait here while I go park the rig."

Lori bit her tongue. *If he thinks I'll snap a salute and say "Aye-aye, sir," he's got another think coming.* Without speaking she got out of the truck and moved to where she could pull on the socks and boots.

"Let me help you, miss," one of the men offered. He had graying hair and a weather-beaten face. "Name's Bill. You must be the new schoolteacher."

She took the hand he offered and pulled herself to her feet. Walking toward the boat, she managed not to step out of the boots or drop her bundle of coat, shoes, and hat. "Thanks, I'm Lori Wilson. Do you have children in school?"

Bill grabbed her bundle and tossed it under the deck of the bow, then put his hands under her arms and lifted her up. "Sit on the edge and slide one leg over at a time."

Lori did as he told her, grateful for his help.

"Yeah, we got a boy fifteen. Been keeping up pretty good by correspondence, but sure glad to have you here to help him." Lori saw him eye the boots.

"I didn't have the right kind of boots. I had to borrow some." She felt the flush on her cheeks.

He smiled. His companion called, "Better not let Greg see you making up to his girl."

Her blush turned hot. "I'm not anyone's girl. Mr. Jensen only offered to take me fishing."

"Don't mind Mac, Lori. He's a big tease." Bill waded back to the beach as Greg approached. The three men exchanged advice on the best fishing holes as Greg shoved off.

He looked at Lori without comment. She thought his glare softened a little when he saw her seated in the back by the huge motor. The metal boat had a center control, where Greg stood to run the boat. She noted the smaller motor mounted next to the big one. "Why two motors?"

"Safety measure. If one conks out, you have a backup. Sometimes I use the little one when I'm trolling."

The big motor roared to life. Lori leaned back to enjoy the wind in her face and the breathtaking scenery. Greg edged out of the bay at a slower speed, but as soon as they rounded the protective spit, he opened the motor up. Noise precluded any conversation as they sped over the water. Greg pointed and she looked toward a rocky island. "Seals," he yelled.

Her floppy boots and his abrupt manners were forgotten. Trees grew almost to the waterline. Beaches littered with logs and seaweed looked like they'd never seen the footprints of man. Huge birds circled ever higher over head. *Maybe they're hawks,* she thought, pointing to them.

"Eagles," Greg shouted.

"Wow!" Her voice was a whisper. She counted eight of the majestic birds flying in lazy circles.

Greg cut the speed and took the boat through a channel by some islands. They were hardly moving when he motioned toward an inlet. "River comes in there. Silver salmon will be going up to spawn. Nice pool up here a little ways where we'll cast for a few."

Lori's senses tingled. Pictures could never do justice to this country.

"See that?" He pointed to the bank where grass and rushes were tromped down. "Bears been fishing, too."

A quiver of apprehension scurried down her spine. She glanced at Greg. His huge frame looked strong and protective.

He brought the boat into a small lagoon and turned off the motor. Huge silver fish jumped out of the water and slammed on their sides back into the deep. "What are they doing?"

"The salmon jump and land like that to knock their eggs loose." His voice was soft. Perhaps he saw and approved of her awe. Lori didn't really care what he thought, she told herself. She was too busy trying to assimilate this whole new world.

Greg pulled poles out, preparing to rig them for fishing. "You know how to use one of these?"

Lori looked at the ultralight trout fishing pole. "I used one of those to catch trout. I thought we were fishing for salmon."

"More sporting this way. This line is ten-pound test. We try to see how big a fish we can land with it. Gives the fish a fighting chance. Plus it's a lot of fun," he added. "You ready to try?"

Frantically, Lori tried to remember everything her brother had taught her. Years had gone by since they'd fished and she wasn't sure she could remember what to do. One look at Greg's unsmiling eyes convinced her she'd do it somehow. Getting to her feet in the cumbersome boots, she took the offered pole. She'd show this chauvinist she could fish. "Let me at them." She looked at the lure on the line. "This all you use?"

"It's called a pixie. You watch to see where a fish jumps and cast in the center of the ripple." With that he flicked his wrist and the silver lure plopped in the center of the circle he pointed to. No sooner did it hit the water, then the tip of the limber rod bent double. Lori watched in wonder as he held the fishing pole taut and reeled.

"Grab the net. It's behind me."

Lori lunged forward, losing her balance as she started to walk out of a boot, but she got hold of the net. Righting herself and taking a deep breath, she managed to net Greg's fish. "That's a beauty."

"Must be about ten pounds."

Anxious not to be outdone, Lori cast her line. She missed the spot for which she'd aimed by four feet. "Hey, that was a little far off. Sure you know what you're doing?"

"Of course I do," she snapped, trying not to show her frustration. Setting her mouth in a determined line, she cast again. The hook on the tip of the lure neatly caught Greg's cap and set it in the water. Lori gasped. Greg turned and she forgot to breathe.

His face crinkled in a wide grin, and the ice in his eyes melted. "Very clever trick. I'd ask you to do it again, but I don't have another hat."

Tears of embarrassment welled in Lori's eyes, but before they could fall, she started to giggle. "Shall I swim over and retrieve that one?" She pointed to the floating cap.

"Why don't you reel it in?"

As she cautiously reeled the hat toward the boat, Greg's deep laugh filled the air. "I've had women try to hook me before, but not with a fish hook. Are you always this aggressive?"

Lori sat down with a bump. "I've got to get out of these boots, and no, I'm not usually so aggressive. I do try to be imaginative." She pulled her tennis shoes out, stuffed the heavy socks in the boots, and put them under her seat.

"If you're going to leave that pole down for a minute, it should be safe for me to go back to fishing." He cast his line.

Embarrassment, anger, and frustration raged in Lori. She pulled the tennis shoes on her bare feet. *I may be cold,* she thought, *but at least now I can take a step without falling. Now I'll show this guy I know how to fish.* Silently she flicked her wrist, sending the bait to the spot where a salmon had just jumped. The resulting tug on the pole nearly took her off balance again. Valiantly, she held the pole high and the line taut. More and more line spun off the reel. Now what?

"Come net this fish for me."

"Do it yourself. I'm busy," she growled, still fighting to hold her own against this monster of the deep. She sensed Greg watching her, ready to help her net the fish, and she felt the sweat break out on her forehead as she prayed she wouldn't lose it.

"You take too long. I'm going back to fishing."

Lori ignored him. Each time she got the fish close to the boat, it pulled away again, causing the reel to spin off line. She didn't have time or energy to argue with Greg.

At last, after what seemed like hours, the fish came in as she reeled. "Could you please net this for me?"

"Finally got one, huh? You've been messing around for fifteen minutes. I've caught two more," Greg teased as he bent over the side with the net. He scooped deep and flopped the huge silver fish into the boat.

"Wow!" they said together.

"My first salmon."

"Get the scales." Greg pointed to his tackle box. "This baby's a record breaker."

He hooked the fish on the scales by its mouth and held it up so he could read the numbers. "Can't be right."

"What's it weigh?" Lori asked.

"Got to do this again. Scales must be broken."

"I suppose I broke the scales, too." Lori wanted praise, not sarcasm.

"Must be right." His voice held a note of wonder. "Nineteen pounds, two ounces." He turned to Lori, and this time there was no doubt of his respect. "The derby fish for all Kodiak waters last year weighed seventeen something. You've got a winner, girl."

"Derby, what derby? I don't even have a fishing license."

He grinned. "You mean I get to claim it?"

Lori hated him at that moment. "No way! I fought that fish, landed it, and it's mine."

Greg dropped the fish in the bottom of the boat and grabbed Lori in a bear hug. "Hey, world, it's Lori's fish," he shouted till the shorebirds rose in fear. He looked down, his face still crinkled in a smile, his hands still on her shoulders. "You are a feisty one. You land a nineteen-pound fish on a ten-pound test line and you're too honest to let me enter him in the derby. I like that." With a final pat on the back, her ordered, "Get back to fishing, woman. One fish won't fill the freezer."

Lori looked into the clear, still water of the lagoon. Hundreds of big fish swam below them. She grabbed her pole and went back to the business at hand. Greg had three and she had one.

Before the evening ended, he had eight and she had six. She and Greg had developed into a team. Without speaking, they knew when the other needed a fish netted. The silence was broken only by the splash of the jumping fish and the screams of the seagulls.

"Time to start back." Greg started to dismantle his fishing

rod. "Better put your boots back on. We'll stop and clean the fish on the way in."

Not even the big boots could spoil her mood. Her cold feet welcomed the warm socks. Bringing in fourteen fish had also brought in water. The bottom of the boat was wet and her tennis shoes were soaked. By the time she had her feet properly clad, Greg pulled the boat up on a sandy shore. She watched as he jumped over the side of the boat and set the anchor in the sand.

Coming back to the boat, he pulled burlap sacks from the bow. "I'll hold these open and you can toss the fish in," he instructed her.

Somehow his words didn't sound so much of a command, Lori thought, as she carefully transferred the fish, some from a five-gallon bucket and some from the bottom of the boat. Greg carried the heavy sack to a large log on the beach.

Cautiously, Lori rolled out of the boat like Bill had shown her. Her left leg went over and the boot slipped almost all the way off, but as she jumped off the side of the boat, she was able to wiggle her foot back in place. She scuffed up the beach toward Greg. "Don't cut the head off my big fish. Got to send a picture of that to my brother," she told him as he tossed a fish on the log and pulled out his knife.

"Doesn't your father fish?"

"My parents were killed in an accident when I was seventeen."

Greg looked up suddenly, but Lori couldn't read his expression. Just as quickly, he went back to gutting fish. "This one's a female." He pointed to the skein of eggs.

Lori looked around. The beach rose toward a dark, towering, primeval forest. "Isn't this polluting?" She pointed to the fish guts Greg threw over the log.

"Cleanup committee is waiting." He waved toward the trees nearest the beach.

At first Lori could see nothing, but then a white head moved, and she spotted three eagles watching them. "Do bears eat them, too?"

Greg nodded his head. "But you're safe." He patted the gun holster lying on the log. He had grabbed it along with the burlap bags from the bow of the boat. "Always carry a nickel-plated 44. Hope I never need it, but better to be safe."

"Does everybody do that?" Lori shuddered at the thought of having to handle a gun.

"No." Greg carried another fish to the water to wash, then put it in the waiting sack. "But anyone who spends time in the woods carries some kind of gun. The black bears will run, but you can't trust the big Kodiak browns. You'll hear some hideous bear tales about them."

A tremor of fear raced down Lori's spine. This place isn't paradise after all.

Greg finished cleaning the fish and sorted them into burlap sacks. "Better get started. It will be dark before we get to the shrimp pots."

"Oh," Lori groaned. She'd forgotten about the shrimp. Carefully she waded out and bumped unceremoniously over the bow of the boat. She nearly lost her balance and fell in the water when she had to grab for a slipping boot. Stifling the cry of fury in her throat, she stepped out of the cumbersome footwear and climbed to her seat in her socks. Greg offered no help or comment, but calmly started the motor when she sat down. She threw the boots under her seat.

Dusk painted the sky in pinks deepening to purple. The colors glowed over the water as they made their way back to camp. Only the motor broke the silence, and Lori found herself wishing they were in a canoe slipping through this unspoiled grandeur. Her reverie came to a halt when Greg turned the corner, past the spit leading to the shelter of the bay. He slowed the boat and coasted toward a large white buoy.

"Can I help?' she asked politely as Greg grabbed the rope connected to the buoy.

"Got about two hundred feet of rope to pull," he panted, as he held the rope taut and rested for a moment.

Lori watched and prayed, *Please Lord, no shrimp*. The pot

emerged. Her heart sank and her stomach squirmed at the sight of the wiggling greenish-gray mass.

"Hand me that bucket."

Lori jumped to grab the white plastic pail Greg indicated. She'd obeyed his order without thinking. Hot anger helped to warm her cold feet when she realized she'd jumped to do his bidding. "Arrogant beast," she muttered half aloud.

"Be a feast all right." Greg dumped the shrimp into the bucket and proceeded to bait the trap with fish heads he'd saved.

Lori cringed from the bucket. She pulled the boots over her wet socks while Greg lowered the shrimp pot back into the water. As the boat approached the shore, she reached for her tennis shoes.

"Leave your stuff in the boat. I'll get the trailer and pull the boat back to my place. You can get your shoes then."

She looked up with a gleam of hope. Maybe he'd forget they were supposed to cook the shrimp.

Her mind dwelled on cooking shrimp and how cold and numb her feet felt. She swung her left leg over the side of the boat and started the right one after it, but as she hit bottom, the rocks under her feet rolled and she fell with a splash. The frigid water stunned her.

Within seconds, Greg stood over her, offering his hand to pull her up. She felt stupid, clumsy, and freezing. "You okay?" He stayed by her as she made her way to dry land.

She nodded, not trusting her voice. She didn't even look at him, fearing tears of frustration would fall. He wrapped his jacket around her shoulders. That did it. She felt six years old again and it was her brother who picked her up and carried her home after she'd fallen off the dock. She looked up to thank Greg, wishing he were Bob, ready to carry her home again.

He still held the jacket around her as he gently asked, "May I buy you a new pair of boots?"

"Boots! What happened to those boots? I borrowed them from Theresa." She tore herself out of the jacket and started for the beach.

"I can see them from here," he told her, pulling the coat back around her. "Now will you stand still while I go get the truck?"

Dear Lord, why am I such an idiot? She watched Greg wade out, retrieve Theresa's boots, and toss them in the boat. Then he jogged to where he'd left his truck.

Quietly and efficiently, he first tucked her into the cab and then expertly backed the truck and trailer toward the water. He jumped out, winched the boat onto the trailer, and started up the hill. With the truck heater going full blast, Lori still shivered. Her dignity lay in shambles, but at least the feeling had started to come back in her frigid feet.

Greg drove up to their side-by-side trailers. "You get into some dry clothes and come over. We'll have something to eat and divide the fish."

She squared her shoulders, set her mouth in a determined line, and opened the door of the truck. "It'll only take me a minute to change and I'll come help you."

four

Lori let the hot water cascade down her back. Slowly, her cold feet regained feeling and her hot embarrassment cooled.

"Wonder where I put the film for my camera?" she murmured, toweling herself dry. "Got to send pictures of my fish to Bob and Priscilla." Thoughts of home dispelled some of her discomfort. She put on a pair of gray flannel slacks, a red sweater, and left her hair in the single braid. She brushed back stray ends of hair that had worked loose and applied fresh lipstick.

A glance at her watch told her a half hour had elapsed. Hastily, she pulled on a pair of sport socks and shoved her feet into clogs. "I'll worry about pictures tomorrow."

She slipped out her back door and across to Greg's wanagan. The door stood open a crack and Marmalade peeked out as Lori came up the steps. When Greg called "Come in," the cat scooted back down the hall and Lori opened the door.

The air smelled strong of fish. She noted the steaming kettle when she entered the kitchen. A wave of shyness flooded her as she sat down in the kitchen chair he waved to. *A bachelor's pad. . .I've never been in a single man's home before.* Thoughts tripped over themselves as she looked around.

"Warm now?"

"Yes," she answered quietly while she watched him scoop bright pink shrimp from the boiling water.

"Here, try some of these." He set the bowl next to a small skillet of melted butter on the table, then turned back to the bucket on the floor. In fascinated horror, Lori watched him grab the long things out of the bucket, snap them in half, and drop one piece in the boiling pot and the other in a second bucket. Marmalade put his front paws on the edge of the bucket and looked in. "Go talk to Lori, you beggar. Maybe she'll peel one for you."

"You feed your cat shrimp?" Visions of fancy cocktail prawns on ice with the accompanying fancy price flashed through Lori's mind as she took a shrimp from the bowl.

"Sure. Have to shoot at least one deer a year just to feed old Marmalade." Greg swung a chair out and sat down across from her. "How do you like them?" he asked as Lori popped a pink morsel into her mouth.

"Mmmm, better than lobster." She reached for another one and laughed as Marmalade put a large paw on Greg's free hand.

"Okay, okay, buddy, don't be so impatient."

Lori relaxed, peeled and ate shrimp, and looked around her. Greg's trailer looked like her own, but his touch was evident. Pictures of wild animals adorned the walls. In one corner of his living room stood a wooden cabinet. Soft music came from the stereo equipment there. Shelves not filled with musical components were filled with books.

She looked back to him when Greg's gaze apparently followed her and he said, "Not much to do around here. The radio is a link with the outside world, while the books and music remind me I don't have to live in it."

"Don't you have a family?"

"Kalissa." He glanced up from feeding the cat another shrimp. "Folks died when I was seven. . .She raised me."

"Accident?"

"Yeah." Absently he peeled another shrimp. "My dad had a fishing boat. Cook took sick, so Mom left me with Kalissa and went to sea with him as his cook. Setting crab pots close to land and got caught in a willawas."

"What's that?" Lori pictured some horrible monster.

"Freak wind. Can sweep down to snap a boat like firewood."

She shuddered. "This country is so wild. Bear attacks, freak winds, what else?"

He stared into space. Lori couldn't read his expression. The only sound was Marmalade's purr. "Down south it's cars, lunatics with guns, and gangs." He looked at her, his blue eyes sad. "There the danger is from man; here we only fight nature. . .Survival. . .that's the way of the world." He stood up, breaking the melancholy mood. "Want some more?"

Lori patted her tummy. "I must have eaten two dozen. I'm full."

"You like tea?"

"That would taste good. What can I do to help?"

"Go sit in the other room. I'll put water on to boil."

Lori relaxed with her head against the back of the couch, listening to the music.

"You take anything in your tea?"

Startled she answered, "Oh. . .uh. . .no thank you."

He sat down in the easy chair and Marmalade promptly curled up in his lap.

She sipped her tea. Looking through the many plants in the front window, she could see the indigo sky. Soon stars would appear. The quiet lay comfortably around them.

"It's so peaceful here," she sighed.

"In spite of the dangers?"

Lori thought about what he'd said earlier. "A different kind of danger. At home we get lots of snow, cold, wind, but it's car accidents and violent crime we fear."

"Don't get much snow here. The wind will blow the rain so hard it comes in sideways and feels like it goes right through you. If the elements don't get you, the loneliness will."

"You get lonely?" Lori asked over the top of her mug of tea.

His look was distant. "Don't have time," came his flip answer. His eyes reflected a sadness that told her he lied.

Greg sat up abruptly, sending the cat scurrying. "You got any room in your refrigerator?"

Lori suppressed a grin as she thought of her nearly empty refrigerator. "Haven't had time to stock up much."

"You can keep your fish cold tonight and take care of them tomorrow. Got any freezer paper?"

She shook her head, making a mental note to add it to the list she'd started.

"I buy it by the case. I'll give you some to wrap your catch in."

"You didn't cut up my big one, did you?" she asked in alarm.

"No," he grinned. "You going to have it stuffed to hang on the wall?"

Her face felt hot at his teasing tone. "I want to take pictures to send Bob."

"He fish a lot?"

Lori thought of her sister-in-law and bitterness rose in her throat. "Not since he got married."

"You don't approve of marriage?"

His question surprised her. "Sure, it's just. . .I don't know. Well, the truth is my brother's wife is dumb."

"Hmmm." He sipped his tea without comment.

Lori stumbled as she tried to describe Priscilla. "Bob and I did just fine till she came along."

"You pretty close to your brother?"

"He's five years older and he's always been my protector." She smiled to herself as pictures crowded her mind of the many adventures they'd shared. "I was seventeen when the folks died. He gave up his apartment in the city and moved home. He kept things going while I finished high school." She put her mug down before continuing quietly. "Guess when I went to college, the big house seemed lonely for him. In my junior year he married Priscilla."

"And you don't like her."

Lori squirmed. "Oh, she's so domestic. Always fussing and never has an original thought."

"Your brother happy?"

She looked at Greg's impassive face and wondered why she was telling him the story of her life. "Yes. . .that's why I'm here."

"You lost me."

"You're right. I don't like Priscilla," Lori admitted. "But Bob loves her. She fusses over him like a simpering idiot and drives me nuts. My friend in Anchorage sent me notices about teaching jobs here and I ran away from home."

"Sorry you came?"

She picked up the mug, accepted a refill, and cradled the warm cup in her hands. "I don't think so. So far, I've found out I've got a lot to learn, but I'm not afraid. This land is exciting."

"I'll remind you of those words next winter when it's rained for twenty days and no plane's been in for over a week." He grinned and petted Marmalade.

A deep and very different feeling crept through Lori's bones. "I won't swear to it yet, but I think it will take more than rain and no mail to send me screaming back to bright lights and crazy people." She felt as contented as Marmalade appeared to be. She watched as Greg ran his hands over the sleeping cat. *He must have a gentle side, too,* Lori thought. *Maybe we can be friends.*

"Are you okay after your dunking?"

She sat up, fighting to keep the flush from her face. "I'm fine," she stammered, embarrassed by his attention. She glanced at her watch. "Wow, it's after midnight."

"You must be tired and I'm keeping you up." Greg moved and Marmalade jumped down, twitching his tail, obviously perturbed at his master's change of mood.

Lori got up from the couch. "Greg, it's been wonderful. This land is beyond description and I'll never forget catching a nineteen pounder." She stretched her arms with her hands clasped in front of her. "You're probably right. There'll be days when I'll be lonesome, but right now I'm positive the days I love this place, the people, and the children will far outnumber the days when I'm ready to go back to what is known as civilization."

His eyes shone in the soft light. He took her hands that seconds before had been stretched in front of her. "I hope your dreams are real. I don't want to see you hurt." His deep, soft voice filled the room.

Lori watched his face, those eyes that sometimes seemed frozen and now sparkled. She pulled her hands back. "Thanks,

Greg. I've had a wonderful evening."

He followed her down the hall and watched as she slipped into her clogs. Marmalade looked at them and went out the open wanagan door with a haughty flip of his tail.

"We'll go fishing again soon," Greg said, as Lori walked the few steps back to her own home.

❧

Lori woke and stretched luxuriously. The clock showed she hadn't slept the morning away and would have time to settle her home properly.

Her small radio didn't offer the variety of Greg's stereo system, but KVOK came in clear. As she dusted, polished, and put the final bits and pieces of her personal things away, she listened to the messages read for the fishing boats. "It's so different. Not survival, like Greg says. . .this is living as it was meant to be." Lori hummed with the radio until she heard a timid knock at her back door.

"Hi, Peggy. How are you today?"

"Fine, thanks," Peggy answered quietly. "Mommy says the ladies will set up for the potluck at three today. Will you come?"

"Oh, it's Friday. Sure I'll be there." She patted Peggy's dark curls. "Want to come in for a while?"

"Mommy said I had to come right back." Her big eyes peeked around Lori into the house.

Lori bent down to hug Peggy. "I'll be at the schoolhouse at three and I'll ask your mom to let you come visit me, okay?"

The child's quick smile told Lori she'd guessed right. The oldest child in the family could use a little quiet time and extra affection now and then.

She watched the little girl skip back down the hill and thought about what to bring to the potluck. She turned to go back in the house and tripped over a cooler. "What's this?" She opened the top to find big slabs of salmon fillet topped by her nineteen-pound fish with head and tail still intact.

"Oh, I forgot the fish." She picked up the note taped to the side of the box.

> *You weren't up so left your fish here. Freezer*
> *paper and tape on the shelf in my wanagan. Help*
> *yourself.*
>
> *Greg*

Might as well get it taken care of, she thought as she slipped on her clogs and went to Greg's. She looked at the shelves in his wanagan with wonder. "Wow! Looks like the corner grocery store." Neatly stacked cans of everything from fruit and vegetables to cartons of Real Fresh milk were there.

She picked up the milk and read the label. Theresa had told her how milk came packaged in containers that sealed out bacteria and kept the unopened contents sweet indefinitely. "Mmm, so that's what it looks like," Lori muttered, thinking of the carton of milk she'd ordered. By the time it got from the dealer to the store to her, the pull date had expired. When she'd tried to pour milk on her breakfast cereal, it came out in sour chunks. "Still think this place should come with a set of instructions." She put the Real Fresh down and picked up the large roll of white paper and tape she figured was meant to wrap fish.

When she walked back to her wanagan, she looked in her freezer to make sure it was plugged in and cold. It took a few tries, but she soon managed to cut the slabs of pink fish into small amounts she could cook for herself. "When I learn to cook," she told herself, carefully wrapping the fish and dropping the packages into the bottom of the freezer.

"Going to take a lot to fill that cavity," she said, looking at her few small packages at the bottom of the large freezer. "Guess I better dig up my pioneer spirit and fill up the larder for winter. Right now I have to do something with this monster." She carried her big salmon to the kitchen table and went for her camera.

"Hmmm, needs perspective." Lori put a ceramic honey pot Priscilla had made for her next to the fish. She snapped pictures from all angles. *Wish I could send the whole salmon to*

Bob and Priscilla, Lori thought. She remembered Priscilla canning fruits and vegetables in her mother's kitchen. "Maybe I could can some and send it to them," she said, putting the honey pot with its little bee on top back in the cupboard. *That dish is cute,* she admitted, shutting the cupboard door. *Maybe Priscilla's smarter than I give her credit for. At least she'd know what to take to a potluck supper.*

"Wait a minute." Lori pulled the door open again. "This should do it." She pulled a box of cake mix left by the last tenant off the shelf. "At least I can follow these directions."

While the cake baked, she wrapped her big fish in plastic garbage bags and put it in her refrigerator. Pride made her wish she knew how to cook it whole so she could take it to the potluck. She shrugged. "Should be enough that I caught it," she scolded herself.

By 2:30 the cake cooled on the shelf, her house was clean and tidy, and Lori went to change her clothes. She put on a blouse and slacks and brushed her hair back into a neat bun. As she applied a light touch of lipstick, she prayed fervently, *Please, Lord, let them like me. I've got a lot to learn about this place and I'll need their help.*

Lori's heart beat faster as she slipped into tennis shoes and walked to the school. Mark and Peggy spotted her and came running to claim her. Half a dozen other children watched from the schoolhouse steps. Joy flooded Lori, and she held out her arms to the children. She stooped to hug Peggy and Mark before taking their hands, and with a child on each side, she strolled to meet her students. Peggy's voice held a note of pride as she told Lori each child's name.

"Hi, I'm Miss Wilson." Lori shook hands with each one and asked their age. "We're going to have a great time in school this year."

Theresa poked her head out the door. "Peggy. Oh, hi, Lori. I was just going to send Peggy after you."

"She's been introducing me to my students." Lori's hand lay softly on Peggy's shoulder.

"Wel,l come on in and meet their mothers." Theresa swung

the door wide to let Lori through.

The hours flew by in a frenzy of trying to keep names and faces straight. Setting the room up with tables and chairs took little time with so many hands to help. Lori met Bill's wife Betty and their son Scott. The tall, shy teenager put up tables and chairs with quiet efficiency.

"He'll be going into Kodiak next year to finish high school," Betty told her. "We want him to have at least one year in a regular school."

"I'll do all I can to prepare him," Lori promised.

"He can use your help in school, but it's getting along in society we worry about. He's pretty shy."

The overwhelming responsibility of the job she'd taken hit Lori. "I'll do what I can," she whispered.

Women and children came and went, and by the time the men started coming in from work at six, food appeared in great quantities.

"I've never seen salmon fixed so many different ways," Lori told Theresa, who stayed by her, helping Lori figure out which men, women, and children made up the families on the island.

"You'll have to get the cookbook the fishermen's wives put out. It'll give you all kinds of ways to fix seafood."

"Could I can salmon?"

"Sure. I've got a canner and we can work together."

"I'd like to send some to my brother and his wife."

"Liz has a tin canner. We'll borrow it and do up a batch. Make a great Christmas present."

"Tin canner?"

Theresa shook her head in wonder. "You know. . .tin cans. Easier to ship than glass."

Lori threw up her hands. "So help me, before I leave this place I'm going to write a book of instructions for newcomers."

Theresa swung Katie up from her booster chair. "We all had to learn and we'll help you till you learn the ropes. Now I've got to get my brood home to bed. Have you seen Mark?"

"Over there getting more blueberry pie. Can't blame him. It's delicious."

"Lots of blueberries in the flat this year."

"Really? Where's that?"

"Over the ridge behind the school," Theresa called over her shoulder as she went after her son.

An hour later Lori trudged up the hill carrying her cake dish and thinking about all the friendly people she'd met. The lights were on in Greg's trailer, but he hadn't joined in the potluck. *I could stop and thank him for filleting the fish. Better not be so forward.* She went on to her own back door.

&

The next morning the sun greeted her again. "I don't believe all the stories of fog and rain," she murmured, opening the drapes to a bright new day. Fixing breakfast and cleaning up her mobile home took only a short time. *I'll start lesson plans when the promised rain shows up. Now I'm going to get pictures of this place to send home,* she told herself.

Her hair stayed neat in a single braid down her back. She wore jeans and a sweatshirt as she slipped the strap of her camera over her shoulder and started out the door. "Hmmm . . .why not?" she said half-aloud, picking up a small plastic pail she'd used as a scrub bucket the day before. "Might see some berries."

From the bluff in front of her house, she snapped pictures before starting down the hill toward the other end of camp. Stopping to take a picture of the school, she set the pail down and spotted a small footpath behind the school. She followed the path into the woods, marveling at the huge mossy areas under the trees. Some trees had grotesque moss formations clinging to them, and she stopped to take a picture of one that looked like a creature from outer space.

Lost in wonder, she had no idea how far she'd gone when she reached the top of the hill and saw the path leading down to an open area. Apparently this had been logged off and now blueberries and small trees grew in profusion. Lori bounded down the path and started filling her bucket with the luscious blue fruit. She moved from one bush to the next and her delight grew as the mound of berries in her pail increased. Picking, feeling the warm sunshine, and thinking about the people she'd met, Lori felt peace.

A muffled snort brought her abruptly back to the world around her. Looking up, Lori's blood froze, and her heart forgot to beat. Thirty yards away stood the biggest bear she'd ever seen. Terror raced ahead of the warnings echoing in her mind. Greg's words came back clearly. . .*Don't go off the main road or more than a mile from camp in either direction.*

Fear held her to the ground. *Run!* her mind screamed, but her feet would only inch slowly backward. The bear stayed on all fours, staring at her. His brown fur shown in the sun and his muzzle dripped blueberry juice.

She'd almost reached the path when she heard a sound behind her. Panic blotted out all reason. She whirled to face this new danger and saw Bill and Betty's son, Scott, calmly aiming a shotgun at the bear. Deafened by the blast, she felt the scream, but did not hear it.

The boy stood still, not speaking for what seemed an eternity. Slowly, fearfully, her eyes followed his gaze. The bear reared up on his hind legs, stared back at them, then dropped to all fours and lumbered off.

"It's okay, miss." He put his arm around her.

Lori shook until her teeth rattled. Turning to bury her face against the shoulder of the slender young man, tears started to course down her cheeks. She felt him take the handle of the bucket she still clutched in her hand.

"You, ah. . .you want to start back now?"

She swallowed hard and tried to stand alone on her shaking legs. Through the blur of tears, she saw the blond youth looking at her while gently urging her back up the path.

"Scott. . .how did you find me. . .how did you know?" Her voice sounded tight and unnatural to her ears.

"I was playing cribbage with Jim. Peggy came and told us you'd gone up this path alone."

"Little Peggy?"

"Yeah, kids know about bears and she knew you shouldn't go off alone."

His tone held no accusation, but hot flames of embarrassment washed over Lori. "How could I be so dumb. A seven-year-old sent out the rescue party."

"Most times bears will just wander off, but you did right not to run or scream. Backing up quiet was the right thing to do."

"Terror kept me from doing anything else." Her composure improved with each step and she looked again at the boy who walked the path ahead of her, gun in one hand, bucket of berries in the other. "Thank you for saving me."

He grinned over his shoulder. "Next time you want to pick berries, let me know ahead of time." He swung the gun onto his shoulder. "This is a pretty good bear gun. Won't kill them, but it's loud and scares them off."

"You've shot them before?"

"Not by myself. I went with my dad last year when he shot one. He has a 7-millimeter to hunt bears. This is just a sawed-off 12-gauge shotgun loaded with buckshot."

"I don't know anything about guns. I'm only thankful that bear decided not to take a closer look at yours."

They came over the hill and saw several women standing in front of the schoolhouse. Scott's mother hurried forward. "Everything all right?" Betty asked him.

"Fine. Miss Wilson got a bucket of blueberries." He handed the pail back to Lori.

Lori looked from one to another. She could feel the salt from her tears on her cheeks and knew she must look a sight. A small figure burst from behind the adults and hurled herself at Lori. Kneeling to embrace Peggy, she told the watching women, "I've behaved like a fool and these two youngsters have saved me."

Scott stood on one foot and then the other and suffered the public hug from his mother when Lori recounted what had happened. She still knelt in the dirt with her arm around Peggy. "I came here to teach them and instead they've taught me."

"You going to make jam?" Peggy asked.

Life goes on, Lori thought. "I don't know how." She looked in the faces of the women around her. "If these kids keep showing me how little I really know, I may have to go home."

"Jam's no big deal. Let me show you," Sandy offered.

"May Peggy come with me?" Lori asked Theresa.

"You sure you're okay?"

"Probably won't stop shaking for another week."

The laughter broke the tension. Stories of bears and recipes for jam filled the chatter as mothers, friends, and children wandered back to their homes.

"Let's stop by my place and get some fruit pectin and wax," Sandy said, heading for one of the trailers in the row by O'Briens'.

Scott had disappeared as soon as the people started moving. Lori looked for him as she walked between Peggy and Sandy. The young woman looked younger than Lori and spoke with a vivacious manner. "Isn't this place awful? Steve promised me a trip to Hawaii if I'd stick it out for a year. Three more months and we're out of here."

Lori gave up looking for the boy and took Peggy's hand. "It's not so bad," she said to Sandy.

"After being stalked by a bear, you can say that? You must be out of your mind."

Lori smiled. "Maybe I am. If not, I soon will be."

Peggy watched quietly as Lori and Sandy measured the berries and sugar and put the jam to boil. "This is easy once you know how. Where did you learn to cook?" Lori asked Sandy.

"Grew up on a farm in Idaho. Always helped in the kitchen."

"My mother loved to cook, so I did housework and she ran the kitchen. After she died, my brother took over. I never did learn to do more than read the directions on a TV dinner."

"It's fun. You'll practice cooking so much around here you'll gain at least fifteen pounds before Christmas."

"Starting now," Lori predicted as the three of them ate bread and jam and drank tea.

"A real tea party," Peggy said, sipping her sweetened tea and milk.

"As long as the Mad Hatter doesn't show up," Lori added.

"What's that?" the child asked.

"A story I'll read you."

"The kids are going to love you. Most of the mothers go stir crazy trapped inside with kids all the time. At least those of us who aren't tied down play games and cards to pass the time. Do you play pinochle?"

"Used to play with my parents years ago."

"We'll get you in a game soon."

"When will you read the story?" Peggy asked.

Lori laughed. "My social calendar is filling up. Thanks to Peggy, the bear didn't cut it short."

Sandy glanced at her watch. "Got to go. Men quit early on Saturday and Steve will be home."

Lori sent Peggy home with a jar of the new jam and spent the next hour cleaning her kitchen. She'd gone to get some aspirin for a headache, when she heard a knock at the back door. Putting the aspirin bottle down on the bathroom counter, she hurried to answer the door.

Greg stood glowering down at her. "You're a little fool!"

"Won't you come in?" Lori said sweetly, trying to mask the instant anger that filled her.

"No."

"You just going to stand there and growl?" The pain that had started to creep up the back of her neck as soon as Peggy and Sandy left now pounded off the top of her head.

"Are you okay?" Greg's tone lost some of its edge.

"No," she snapped.

"What's wrong?" His eyes went wide with fear. "They told me the bear ran off."

"He did. Are you going to run, too, or will you come in?"

He appeared to relax slightly and looked at his heavy work boots. She followed his gaze. "Don't worry about them. Come in."

He followed her down the hall. "Want some tea?" She didn't

wait for an answer, but put the tea kettle on the stove.

Greg pulled out a kitchen chair and sat down. "What's wrong? Did you get hurt?"

"You're right. I acted like a fool. I've been scared out of my wits and now my head aches till I can't see straight." She plopped in a chair across from him.

A faint grin softened his features. "Did you get a picture of him?"

She moved the camera back and got up to get cups. "Are you kidding? I was so scared I couldn't move."

He took her hand and pulled her back to the table. "Sit down and tell me what happened."

"I started out to take pictures, saw the berries, and got carried away. Peggy spotted me going off alone and told Scott, who came looking for me. There you have it. Dumb schoolmarm saved by smart kids."

He still held her hand in his. She pulled it back. "Guess it's true that the Lord takes care of fools and newcomers."

five

"That man is impossible!" Lori slammed the book shut and pushed her chair away from the desk in her converted office. She jumped up and stormed to the window of what had been the extra bedroom. "I can't concentrate on lesson plans." She looked out at the wisps of fog floating in and out of the dripping branches of the forest. "It isn't the rain and gloom." She turned back to pace the four steps between her desk and the window. "He's maddening." She flung her hands in the air. "Acts like he's worried about me one minute and yelling at me like I was an errant child the next."

Why do you let him bother you?

She sank into the desk chair. Her elbows on the desk, she supported her chin with her hands. "Lord, do I have to be friends with everyone?"

The bear incident remained the talk of the camp, with Greg being the only one to point out it was her own fault.

You never heard him say you were dumb in public. Are you sure it isn't your guilt that causes this anger?

She remembered the night he'd come to her house, first to scold her and then to console her. *I must have been dreaming.*

Oh, we'll never be friends, and I'll never figure out how to teach a dozen kids on a dozen different levels.

You could get a job on a fishing boat, she continued the argument with herself.

She smiled at the wall in front of her. *I did get a lot of attention over my nineteen-pound silver.* A neat stack of gold-colored cans were on the shelf in her wanagan and pictures winged their way to Bob. She sighed.

A knock at her back door broke into her reverie. Lori padded down the hall in her sock feet. Four freshly scrubbed faces waited on her doorstep.

"Good afternoon, Miss Wilson," four little girls said in unison.

"Come in, ladies. It must be time for tea." Lori made an elaborate bow, and her young friends giggled as they pushed each other along the way to her kitchen.

Peggy, Debbie, Missy, and Callie ranged in age from seven to nine. Construction paper and pencil sketches had created invitations. Today's agenda included tea and another chapter of *Alice in Wonderland*. Tomorrow's group would be the kindergarten set.

Sandy's prediction had proved right: Lori was learning to cook. Cookies were laid out on a pretty plate and teacups waited for the little girls, who eagerly tried to behave like grown-up ladies between giggles.

Sandy dropped by partway through the party. "Just wanted to remind you Bible study's at my house Thursday night." She looked at the assembled little girls and their cups of tea. "I knew you were nuts. A tea party on Monk's Island?"

"If the kids have something to look forward to, it makes their lives more fun."

"Hmmm, I look forward to anything different. Maybe you're right. Sure you aren't getting paid to baby-sit?"

"The kids have to eat the stuff I cook. That's the catch."

Sandy laughed and went off to remind others of the Bible study.

Time passed quickly. The cookies were reduced to a few crumbs. The last cup of spilled tea had been wiped up and Alice escaped the Red Queen. Peggy, Debbie, Missy, and Callie trooped off for home, and Lori surveyed her kitchen.

She washed cups, swept up crumbs, and hummed along with the radio. "Greg may not like me, but the junior set thinks I'm okay," she said under her breath.

Later that evening, Lori went out to sit on the log in front of her trailer. The fog hung heavy over the calm water. An eagle screamed in the distance. The cool air sent a chill down her spine, and she hugged her jacket around her in the damp mist. A light breeze rippled across the bay and played with the wisps of hair around her face.

Marmalade looked around the corner of Greg's trailer, paused, then strolled importantly to the other end of the log. He and Lori exchanged looks. The big orange cat hopped on the log, sat down, and with a final flick of his whiskers in her direction, proceeded to groom himself.

Lori sighed in contentment. Her antagonism toward Greg was forgotten. The afternoon had been fun. She knew the mothers of the little girls appreciated the break in routine— *and I get to send them home and soak up the silence,* she thought. She put her feet up on the log and hugged her knees to her chest.

"Maybe it will clear tomorrow."

"You startled me." She looked up to see Greg's rugged countenance above her.

"Sorry, saw you sitting here alone and thought you might like some company."

"I'm not alone." She pointed to Marmalade, who walked the length of the log and arched his back against her hand. She smiled, pleased with the cat's offer of friendship.

Greg's look of astonishment made her giggle like one of her tea party guests.

"Your attack cat has been tamed." She continued to rub the cat's fur as Marmalade butted his head against her hand.

"Never thought I'd see the day. At least the old tom has good taste."

"Why, thank you."

"Things going all right for you?"

"Haven't seen a bear all week."

"I've heard about all the things you're doing with the children." His deep voice caught her attention.

"Can't be all readin', writin', and 'rithmetic." She looked out over the bay. "It's so different here. Going back south will be rough on a lot of them."

"Don't you have it backwards? They'll be going back to TV, movies, greasy hamburgers."

"Stop right there. Only been here a month and I crave those

greasy hamburgers."

Greg's laugh rolled down the hill and echoed back. "See, you're worried for nothing. Kids will adapt. But I'm afraid you're wasting your time."

"Teaching little girls table manners at a tea party is a waste of time?" She spoke in a flat monotone.

"No, I don't mean that. What you're doing for both the kids and their mothers is good." He put a foot on the log and leaned forward, hand on his knee. "I was talking about your desire for a greasy hamburger. Afraid all I can offer you is some ground venison."

"I'll take it, if you'll come for dinner and help me eat it."

He put out his hand. She let her legs drop and reached to clasp it. "You've got a date."

Marmalade stormed back to the other end of the log. Greg pointed to the cat's twitching tail. "I think your boyfriend's jealous."

"He'll get over it."

The dusk turned to darkness earlier now as fall approached. No Indian summer here. Occasional days of sunshine were welcomed as fog and rain became more and more prevalent. Lori walked to Greg's back door and accepted the package of venison. Marmalade allowed her to pat his head one more time before she went home.

The next morning she entertained five little ones. When they went home at lunchtime, she cleaned up her house before running to Theresa to ask for a recipe for meat loaf.

"Why meat loaf?"

"Greg gave me ground venison and I opened my big mouth and offered to cook it for both of us. I don't even own a cookbook."

"So Greg's coming for supper. Sounds cozy."

"That grouch! But I owe him one after he took me fishing and fed me shrimp. When he gave me the venison, I thought I should invite him."

Theresa said nothing, only raised her eyebrows when she looked up from the paper where she was copying the recipe.

"Good thing I'd given the kids today off. The older ones are supposed to be studying for a quiz."

"Aaron and Mark sure had a good time this morning. How come they smell like lemons?"

"The finger paint stained their fingers and I used lemon juice to get it off."

"That's what the old shirts were for."

"Sure. I told you I'd cut the sleeves off and make smocks."

Theresa laughed. "A few of us think only in terms of maternity smocks. You had me worried."

Lori joined in the laughter. "Only paint smocks for this schoolteacher."

Theresa handed her the paper. "How about another cup of coffee?"

Lori waved her hand over her cup. "No thanks. Got to run, clean up the house, and start supper."

"At three o'clock?"

"Don't forget I'm a beginner. Takes me hours, and then everything gets done at different times."

"I don't care how you cook. The joy you bring the kids besides teaching them is fantastic."

"Thanks. I'll feel better about teaching if the teenagers do well on that test tomorrow."

Lori hurried back to her house. Carefully, she laid out all the ingredients. First she made a salad of canned fruit in Jell-O. Fresh salad had become just a memory; she'd learned lettuce usually dripped slime by the time it got to Monk's Island. She scrubbed potatoes and crossed her fingers while she said a quick prayer that they'd be done the same time as the meat loaf.

By six, everything was ready. The oven was on, the salad was firm, the vegetables were in a pan ready to heat, and the table was set. Lori brushed and rebraided her hair, then put on gray flannel slacks and a plaid blouse. Flushed from the heat of the oven, she tossed her sweater back on her bed and went to apply a light touch of makeup.

She'd just put her lipstick away when she heard Greg at the back door.

"Hi."

"Little hard to find flowers this time of year, so I brought you a loaf of bread."

"Wow, did you bake this?" Lori took the loaf of bread.

"I usually bake all my bread. Hey, something smells good."

Lori groaned inwardly as they entered her kitchen. *He can bake bread and I can't boil water.* Trying to smile past her worry, she got out glasses and took a bottle of sparkling apple juice from the refrigerator. "Will you do the honors?"

With a broad smile and a flourish, Greg pulled a Swiss army knife out of his pocket.

"You came prepared for anything. Hope you don't need that knife to cut my cooking."

Her nervousness increased as she put their supper on the table.

"Looks delicious and I'm starved."

It did look good, Lori thought. Her salad had unmolded with no trouble. Her blueberry jam sat in a crystal bowl next to a plate of Greg's homemade bread, the potatoes were done, and the meat loaf gave off mouth-watering smells.

"Will you bless the food?"

Greg scowled, but bowed his head and muttered, "For what we are about to eat, we thank You, Lord."

"Amen and well done."

"Had to do it in college."

"Really?" Lori was curious and about to ask more, but she paused to cut the meat loaf. Her excitement at putting out a good dinner plummeted. She couldn't cut the meat loaf. She glanced at Greg, who was piling butter on his baked potato. Again she pushed the knife into the meat loaf, but it felt like rubber. The knife bounced back. By now Greg watched her.

"Need help? I can cut up game, so cutting a meat loaf should be a cinch." He took the knife and sliced into the meat. His brow furrowed in puzzlement. "What did you put in here?"

"I followed Theresa's directions exactly," Lori cried.

Greg shook his head. "Something's not right—unless you

were trying to invent a substitute for rubber. Let's see those directions."

Lori took the slip of paper from the cupboard and handed it to him. He looked at it and then at her. "You made it just like this?"

She nodded her head. Tears burned her eyes and she didn't dare speak.

Greg looked more puzzled than ever. Lori's embarrassment turned to anger. She banged open cupboards and started pulling out the onions, spices, and tomato soup she'd used. "See, it's all here." She slammed down the oatmeal box. "I even cooked my own and didn't use instant."

"You cooked the oatmeal?" His eyes sparkled and his mouth twitched.

Lori stopped and stared at him. He looked like he might strangle, but he finally roared with laughter. He wiped tears from his eyes. "Lori, Lori, you really don't know how to cook, do you?" he gasped.

"I wasn't supposed to cook it?" she whispered.

Gradually Greg regained his composure. "I'm sorry I laughed," he apologized. "Let's eat the rest of your supper. It looks real good."

"So did the meat loaf," she muttered. Then she brightened. "Go ahead and eat your potatoes while they're hot. I'll open a can of Spam."

By the time she had sliced and fried the Spam, Lori started to feel better. She could laugh with Greg over her attempt to cook.

"Dessert should be okay. I already tried it on the kindergarten crowd this morning." She set bowls of pudding on the table and sat down.

Greg picked up his spoon, looked at the pudding and back at Lori. "Ahh. . .there are swirls of blue stuff in here. Is that blueberries?"

Lori took a bite of pudding. "No, it's finger paint."

Greg's spoon clattered against his glass. "Finger paint!"

It was Lori's turn to laugh. "Come on, I want to show you something." She grabbed his arm and pulled his six-foot, two-inch frame down the hall to her office. "Now see. . .finger paint. I had five kids from three to five, and I gave each of them a piece of freezer paper and put a spoonful of cooked pudding with blue food coloring in it on the paper and presto. . .finger paint. And they got to eat the leftovers."

Greg's laugh filled the trailer. "Lori, you're beautiful. But from now on, I'll do the cooking and you take care of the kids." He looked at the five pieces of art drying on the floor. "Picassos in the making."

His body filled the narrow door. Lori looked up at his rugged features and timidly offered, "The pudding seemed so plain and I thought the blue swirls made it pretty."

"Before or after it was finger paint?" His grin helped her forget the failed meat loaf. He stood back so she could precede him back to the kitchen. "All right, little schoolteacher, let's go eat your pretty pudding."

Lori put the tea kettle to boil and Greg retrieved his fallen spoon.

"It's good," he said after taking a large mouthful of pudding.

Lori put tea in the teapot. "I can do all right if all I have to do is read directions on the box."

"Is that how you learned to make finger paint?"

"Next week it's play dough," she teased.

"You're going to make play dough out of pudding?" he asked incredulously.

"No, out of peanut butter and powdered milk."

He threw back his head, and his laugh resounded off the walls. "You are a wonder."

"But not a very good cook."

He sipped the tea she poured. "Best fried Spam I ever had." He put his cup down. "And you make a good cup of tea."

Lori drained her juice glass before drinking any tea. *We might be friends yet,* she thought. The easy, teasing conversation continued while they washed dishes together.

Greg hung up the dish towel and she reached to fill the tea kettle again. "Let's move into the living room. I don't have good music like you do. Just the radio."

"Radio's fine. I like to hear the weather report at ten."

She turned KVOK on while he poured the tea. He handed her a cup. She curled her feet under her on one end of the couch. Greg held up his cup. "A toast to the best hostess on Monk's." He stretched his frame out in the big chair.

"I'll always be sure to have lots of Spam in the house." She smiled and sipped the tea. "And your homemade bread tasted great."

"Supposed to bring wine and flowers."

"I don't drink."

"Good thing, because alcohol is forbidden on the island."

She remembered George and Shorty at the terminal the day she'd arrived in Kodiak. "You don't let the men have liquor?"

"In this isolation, liquor can be too much temptation."

"I never thought about it."

His look was far away. "Liquor has hurt the natives."

"You care a lot about the native Alaskans, don't you?"

He came back from wool-gathering and smiled at her. "I grew up with them. In many ways, I'm one of them."

Lori smiled in spite of herself. "They're small and dark and you're big and blond."

"I meant I've learned their ways. Learned to work in harmony with nature." He grinned. "Learned not to trust short timers and businessmen in eight-hundred-dollar suits."

"And you think I'm a short timer?"

She couldn't read his look. His eyes held pain. "You're a tourist teacher, a reformer."

"Reformer." Lori sat up in anger. "What have I tried to change?"

He shrugged. "Heard you joined the local Bible study group. Next thing I hear you'll be having Sunday school for the kids."

She swung her feet down and put her cup on the table. "And what's wrong with teaching the Bible? You haven't seen any missionaries in eight-hundred-dollar suits have you?"

His voice sounded quiet, thoughtful. "I grew up in an isolated village surrounded by warm, loving people and incomparable scenery. We had the same basic human values that were taught in most societies—but when I went south to get an education, your Christians treated me like I was a savage to be tamed."

She watched him twist the cup in his hands and heard the sadness in his voice.

"Kalissa taught me more than those hypocrites ever knew."

"Where did you go to school?"

"Seattle. University of Washington."

"And you were treated badly?" she asked incredulously.

"I was seventeen and didn't remember seeing anything bigger than Kodiak. People who'd known my mother wrote to me over the years. They met me at Sea-Tac Airport. Olga. . .well, she knew my mother," he explained. "She tried to be nice, but her daughter Elsa laughed at me." He looked at Lori as if pleading to be understood. "She laughed at my clothes, she laughed at my awe of the city, she laughed when I thought she was beautiful. No one told me sixteen-year-old white girls giggle at everything. Native girls are ready to marry and take care of a house, husband, and babies at that age. Elsa gave me such an inferiority complex, I hated civilization. I was homesick for the village and Kalissa. Oh, I tried religion. The preacher asked me what it felt like to live with savages."

"And where did you meet this great preacher?"

"Olga thought it would be nice if I lived with a family instead of the dorm, so she set me up to room with an old couple. He'd retired from the church and the money I paid made it easier for them."

"Did he always talk like that? I mean, put down your heritage—or rather the heritage you grew up with?"

"He raged most of the time." Greg smiled. "That's what I meant about saying grace. The old guy would ramble on for fifteen or twenty minutes till everything on the table got cold."

"What about his wife?"

"Meek little Sarah never spoke above a whisper. Spent lots of time in the kitchen cooking up huge meals of meat and potatoes."

"Wasn't all bad then."

"Except I grew up on fish and game—and the greasy hamburgers you crave upset my stomach. Didn't help that the old man prayed till the grease on the meat congealed."

"Did you stay there all four years?"

"No. In my junior year, they diagnosed the old man with Alzheimer's. Sarah had to put him in a nursing home and go live with their daughter. I got a place of my own."

"And you still judge Christians by the ravings of a sick old man?"

"It's more than that. My people," he grinned, "I mean, the native Alaskans, have created a culture based on kinship with the spirits of the universe. All I saw in the years I stayed in the south was a culture based on money. They don't worship God, they worship what they can buy. . .material things."

"And you were poor?"

"No!" he thundered. "My parents had insurance on themselves and their boat. Most of that money sits in a trust fund growing until I can buy and sell many of those snobs. I paid my own way, but I never have and I never will join the race to own more than I need. I have luxuries—which I'll always share without some preacher quoting words thousands of years old."

"I live by those words that have survived thousands of years." Lori spoke with passion. "Sounds to me like you still blame civilization because you were a scared, homesick kid. How long ago was it, anyway?"

He looked astonished as he mouthed "ten years" without a sound. He regained his voice. "You sound like Kalissa. She says it's wrong to hold a grudge." His words were soft, in striking contrast to his rage of a moment ago.

"She must be a smart lady. I'd like to meet her."

His outburst dissipated as quickly as it had come. "Maybe you will. Maybe you will." He put his cup down and stood up. "I'm sorry if I upset you."

"Sit down and relax. We have to finish the pot of tea."

He sank back into the chair while Lori went to refill their

cups. "Thank you," he murmured as she handed him his mug.

"You're welcome."

"You're different, Lori."

"Different how? Because I can't cook and I yell at spoiled little boys?"

He grinned. "I deserved that. Tell you what, Dennis and I are going hunting this weekend. I'll bring you some more venison."

"I'll keep practicing. Who knows, I may invent a substitute for making tires." She turned to put the teapot down. He took her free hand gently in his own.

She thought of his lack of faith and pulled away. *Reformer* echoed in her mind. Silently she took her own cup and sat down.

She took a sip of tea. "Friendship is a good thing." Her words fell into the silence.

"I'm not good at polite conversation."

"That's your opinion. I thought we were doing great—except you only think it's proper for me to teach the kids on weekdays."

"You'll never reform me that way."

"Why should I reform you? I like you the way you are," she said, spitting out the word reform.

"You could like me as a native."

"I don't know any natives and I don't know why they are any different. Kalissa sounds like a special person and you were lucky to have her. Just like I was lucky to have Bob when my parents died. You grew up in a different world. That's what I tried to say the other night about the kids in camp. You experienced culture shock. I'd like to help the kids here to prepare for it."

"Why do you care what happens to those kids? All you have to do is teach them to read and write."

"More native psychology?"

"No," he said sharply, "the natives have a great love for children."

"Well, they aren't the only ones. Loving children and

teaching them is my God-given talent and I plan to use it to His glory."

"Maybe we should try politics. We aren't doing so well on religion." He spoke softly.

"Sounds reasonable. What's new at the bunkhouse?"

"No politics there. They only get excited when somebody sends in a new deck of cards."

"Or when you and Whitney get into it over how logging roads should be laid out."

He looked over the rim of his cup as he took a drink. "So you know all the island gossip? Aren't you afraid to have a man in your house? Could start a scandal."

"Liven things up all right. Give the ladies something new to talk about."

"Aren't you afraid of tarnishing your spotless image?"

"Can't happen. I'm only giving a poor savage some lousy meat loaf."

He shook his head and laughed. "I give up. You talk to your kids—and if you find a way I can help, I'll do it."

"Really?" she asked in excitement.

"As long as I don't have to eat finger paint or play dough."

Lori felt her face flush with pleasure and bounded up with a burst of energy. "That's great. I'm giving the teenagers a test tomorrow that should help me not only evaluate what they know, but it should pinpoint their interests. I know you'll be able to help with the teenage boys. They don't like finger paint or play dough either."

Greg rose and put his cup on the kitchen counter. He took hold of her chin and tipped her head back so he could look into her eyes. "You're special."

Puzzled, Lori wondered, *What next?*

Greg sighed and let go of her. "But there's no place in my life for a woman."

Lori stepped back, stunned.

"I'm sorry. I shouldn't have touched you."

"No problem," she said. "I just don't understand where you're coming from. I'm certainly not looking for romance, but I did think we could be friends."

"I hope I haven't offended you." His voice held concern.

Lori's feelings were at war within her. This man dared to question her faith and wondered if he offended her? She took a deep breath before she spoke. "I'm not offended and I hope you'll come again."

"So do I." He retreated to the back door to retrieve his shoes. She watched him as he put them on. "Let me know if I can help with the children."

Before she could gather her wits and speak, he was gone.

six

Lori pushed her personal problems back and concentrated on the children in school. She had four teenagers. Scott was doing eleventh-grade work, Pete tenth-grade, and two were on a junior high level. Scott tested out as her best student. He'd been keeping up by correspondence with a visiting teacher who flew out to the island every four to six weeks. Academ-ically, he caused no worry, but his quiet reserve made Lori remember Greg's story. Scott hadn't been in a regular school in five years. Would he suffer the same as Greg when he moved into a different environment?

Stifling her worried thoughts, she picked up his test paper. The last question instructed the students to write a paragraph about something they were interested in. Again, Lori read the page of boyish scrawl. Scott showed not only an interest, but considerable knowledge of the marine life around the island. *I'll talk to Greg about him. How to get him a scholarship to go on to college will be the next step,* she told herself.

Pete would not be as much of a problem. He'd been in regular school until last year and had already stated he wanted to become a diesel mechanic like his dad.

Lori went over the test papers on her desk again before closing the door on the schoolhouse and starting up the hill toward home. Pride in her students lifted her mood. All of them had done well on the test. She only had one sixth grader who would need extra help. The others had studied independently or with help from their parents, and they had kept up to or ahead of the grade level where they belonged.

The damp air chilled Lori. Shivering, she pulled her hood over her head and decided that as soon as she got home she'd write a note to Priscilla, telling her sister-in-law how much she appreciated the down jacket's warmth.

Priscilla wrote every week. Lori found herself looking forward to the letters. The news of people she'd grown up with, been bored with, glad to get away from now brightened her life on this remote island. Even Priscilla didn't seem so dumb. "At least she can cook," Lori muttered, letting herself in the back door of her mobile home.

There were no lights on at Greg's. He'd gone to Kodiak on business for a week. Marmalade sat in his kitchen window where Lori could see him when she turned on the light over her table. Greg said he left a litter box and lots of food in the wanagan when he went away for a few days.

"Poor kitty looks lonely," Lori said aloud. Impulsively, she went back out, and by the time she opened Greg's back door, Marmalade stood waiting. He arched his back as she rubbed him. "Want to come home with me?" she asked, continuing to pet the cat.

As if he understood her, Marmalade started down the steps and marched toward her home. Lori followed him as he boldly walked into her trailer. She left the door ajar so he could go back out.

"Maybe I can fix your supper better than your master's," she said as she sliced bread and took out milk. She had toast and cocoa while the cat lapped up warm milk. When she curled up on the couch to read, Marmalade snuggled close to her and purred contentedly. "Nice not to be alone, huh, fella?" Lori stroked his back and he purred louder.

The evening passed quickly. Lori read until the lights dimmed and she reached for a candle. "Generator must be acting up," she told her furry friend. "Time to go to bed anyway." Marmalade gave her a polite "meow" and went out the back door. Greg's wanagan door stood slightly open so the cat could get back in to his food.

❧

After school a couple days later, Lori stopped to visit Theresa. She let the children out at 2:30 so there would still be daylight for them to play even when winter found the sun setting at four in the afternoon.

"Dennis says the cranberries are ripe. Want to go berry picking Saturday?" Theresa asked.

"Greg said he and Dennis were going hunting Saturday."

"True, but Sandy said she'd watch the kids for me if I'd help her make cranberry juice."

"You sure you want me along? I attract bears, remember?"

Theresa laughed. "Scott will go with us and pick berries for Betty."

Lori drained her coffee cup. "Okay, but I don't know what to do with them after they're picked. Only cranberries I've ever seen were in a can."

"We'll cook them up together."

"Sounds good. Greg promised me some of the venison they get this weekend. You'll have to teach me to cook that, too."

"No more meat loaf?" Theresa teased.

"Yes! I'm going to make it till I get it right," she giggled, "or invent a rubber substitute."

The women visited a while longer before Lori started up the hill toward home. Marmalade waited for her by the back door.

"Hi, old friend." Lori reached down to stroke the cat's head. "Hope your master isn't mad at me for letting you out."

The cat stood up on his hind feet to butt his head against her hand, begging for attention. His saucer of warm milk had become an expected ritual. His habit of lying next to her on the couch and purring made her evenings more pleasant. At bedtime he would give her a good night meow and go out the back door.

&

Lori heard Hal fly in on Friday afternoon, so she wasn't surprised when Marmalade didn't meet her after school. *Must have gone home to Greg,* she decided, as she put away the groceries Jim had left in the wanagan.

Saturday dawned clear. "Looks like a great day to pick berries," Lori called to Theresa as she pulled off her shoes at her friend's back door. The sound of squeals and giggles told her Sandy already had the children entertained.

"Dennis and Greg were off at daybreak. They should get

three or four deer."

"That many? Isn't there a limit?"

"This year it's five apiece."

"Wow."

"There are so many deer and only so much feed. Winter kill is a lot worse than a quick bullet. Besides, around here we live off the land. That means a lot of fish and game."

"And berries."

Scott arrived at Theresa's door with his gun in one hand and a bucket in the other. "Ready?"

"Sure are." Theresa and Lori pulled on shoes and waved good-bye to the children and Sandy. "You kids behave," Theresa called to her brood.

The berry pickers found lots of the small red fruit. "Not as big as the New England kind," Theresa explained.

"I wouldn't know. I've never picked them before."

By noon their buckets were full and no bears had made an appearance.

"Maybe bears don't like cranberries," Lori said hopefully, as they started back to camp.

"Your dad going to hunt bear again?" Theresa asked Scott.

"I don't think so. He had the skin off the one he got last year tanned. Mom says we'll never have a wall big enough to put in on. Claws on that thing are five inches long."

Lori shuddered. She still had nightmares about bears. "If I never see another bear it will be too soon."

"Mostly it's just stories, Miss Wilson. You're safe," Scott assured her. "Just think, there are no snakes, ants, or poisonous insects here."

"I'll take the ants, you can have the bears," Lori quipped.

Scott left the women with a final wave when they got to camp. "Got to get the berries to Mom," he said as he turned toward his family's trailer.

"He's a nice boy," Theresa said.

"I worry how he'll adapt to civilization."

Theresa giggled. "You mean we're not civilized?"

"Oh, you know what I mean. Betty said they're sending

him into Kodiak to school next year."

"He's going to live with Pastor Johnson, so he'll be in a good home." Theresa set her bucket down on the step of her trailer. "Hey, you going to entertain kids at your place tomorrow?"

"Yes, I'm having the young ones come early and will have the ten and older come later. Too hard to have all ages at once in my little trailer."

Theresa smiled. "Oh, Betty's having a party tomorrow night."

"Want me to watch the kids so you and Dennis can go together?"

Lori saw the quick look of longing before Theresa spoke. "No, then you'd miss a good time."

"You and Dennis go. I'll have fun with the kids." She swung her bucket up on Theresa's top step. "Now what am I supposed to do with these things? That's the price I ask for baby-sitting."

Sandy came to the back door with Katie in her arms. "We're going to make sauce and juice for Thanksgiving punch. Only this year we won't let Theresa near the punch."

"Why?" Lori looked from one woman to the other.

Sandy laughed and Theresa joined in. "First story I heard when we got to camp," Sandy giggled. "Seems last year Theresa made cranberry juice and put it in her fridge until Thanksgiving. She mixed it with orange juice and ginger ale and it was the hit of dinner with the loggers."

Both women broke into gales of laughter. Sandy pointed to Theresa. "You tell her what happened."

"I didn't taste the stuff 'cause I really don't like cranberry juice. We didn't have a clue till all the guys from the bunk-house started drinking the stuff by the glassful. Then Dennis tried it. Seems the juice had fermented in my fridge and my punch packed quite a kick."

Lori joined in the laughter. "I'm glad I'm not the only one to make goofs when it comes to cooking."

"This year we'll freeze the juice until Thanksgiving."

"And disappoint George and Shorty. You gave them a great treat last Thanksgiving from all I hear," Sandy commented.

"I've got lots of room in my freezer. I'd be glad to store it." Lori looked at Theresa. "I'll even make the punch if you'll tell me how."

"Sounds good to me." Theresa took the squirming Katie from Sandy's arms. "Let's get started."

The women spent the afternoon crushing, boiling, and preserving cranberries in sauce, syrup, and juice. The shadows of late afternoon crept in before Lori started home.

Greg had two deer hanging from the rack at the front of his trailer. He deftly skinned the last one as Lori approached. "Hey, Lori, have you seen Marmalade?"

"He's been coming to my place every evening since you've been gone. When he didn't show up last night, I assumed he'd gone home."

"I haven't seen him since I got back."

Lori caught her breath. "Greg, what have I done now? I opened your back door because I thought Marmalade looked lonely and I enjoyed his company in the evening."

Greg stood up and wiped the sweat off his forehead with his shirt sleeve. "It's okay. He's been gone before."

"I hope he's all right." She pointed to the carcasses. "You had good hunting."

"Not bad. Dennis got two for his family. After it has hung for a few days, we'll cut it up and I'll give you some."

"Thanks. I'll keep trying and maybe I can bake you a new set of tires."

"Be hard to do with this meat. It's so tender you'll be able to cut it with a fork." He grinned like a little boy. "I brought you a present from town."

Lori felt the flush sweep over her face. "Really?"

"When I get cleaned up, I'll bring it over."

Shyly she admitted, "I baked some cookies yesterday."

"With leftover play dough?"

"No, Katie ate that. All I have to serve you are chocolate chip cookies."

He'd gone back to skinning the deer and with a final tug pulled the hide free. He looked up. "Hmm, sounds good."

"See you later." Lori went into her trailer. It looked like home now with prints on the walls and plants hanging in the front window. She had more ceramic dishes and bowls of Priscilla's sitting on tables. A large cookie jar sat in the middle of the kitchen table. She often baked cookies so she'd have something to offer the children when they dropped by.

Lori went through her office to the bathroom, peeling off clothes as she went. She loosened her braided hair and stepped into the shower. The hot water cascaded over her tired body as she washed her hair. Getting out, she toweled her hair dry, then wrapped the towel around her body and walked into her bedroom.

"Good grief!" Lori dropped to her knees beside the bed and reached to touch Marmalade.

The big tabby raised his head and meowed feebly. He lay on his side with his mangled and bloody front leg stretched out on her comforter.

Tears stung Lori's eyes. "You poor baby. How did you drag yourself in here? Greg. . .I've got to tell Greg." She jumped up, letting the towel fall to the floor. Wildly pulling clothes out of drawers and closet, she scrambled into jeans and a shirt. She wrapped the wet towel around her dripping hair. All the while she talked softly to the cat.

Running out her back door, she dashed to Greg's, shouting, "Greg, Greg, come quick!" She stopped in his kitchen as he came out of his bedroom wearing only a pair of jeans. His hair dripped onto his bare chest. Without thinking, Lori grabbed his arm and insisted, "Come on, it's Marmalade."

Greg ran across the path in his bare feet. He followed her into the bedroom, then bent over the cat. Marmalade raised his head a little and tried to meow.

"How bad is it?" Lori whispered.

"Looks like he got in some fight." Greg looked around the room. "Wonder how he got in here?"

The blush rushed over Lori's face when she looked at the towel on the floor and scattered clothes where she'd pulled them from drawers in her haste. "I've been letting him in every day. I must have left the door open this morning."

"Your quilt's a mess."

Lori saw the dirt and blood on the bed. "Don't worry about that. What can we do for Marmalade?"

"I'll go get Jim. He's the medic around here."

"I'll stay here with Marmalade." She continued to stroke the cat's head and talk softly to him. After Greg left, she picked up the scattered clothes and brushed out her long, wet hair. When Greg came back, followed by Jim, she was heating milk.

Greg had taken time to put on a shirt and shoes. Lori noticed Jim's puzzled look as Greg directed him into her bedroom.

"What's the cat doin' here?"

"We don't know. I left the door open and found him when I got home. Can you help him?" Lori pleaded.

Jim looked from Greg to Lori without comment and bent to check the injured animal. "Mac said he found a fox up the road a piece. Brought the tail in, but said the pelt was chewed up. Looks like your cat fared a little better."

Marmalade eyed Jim while Lori petted him and whispered to him so he would lie still and let Jim inspect his wound.

"Bad one. . .Got some sulfa powder. We can clean the gash up, put some powder on, and keep it bandaged. You goin' to leave him here?" Jim looked from Greg to Lori.

Lori opened her mouth to speak, but no sound came out.

"He must have been confused when he crawled in here. I'll take him home where he belongs," Greg responded.

"I'll fetch the first aid kit." Jim headed out the door.

"The comforter is already dirty. Let Jim work on him here. Then take him home."

"All right," Greg answered as Jim came back from his truck with a black wooden box.

"Never worked on an animal before. Way you spoil that cat he don't know he ain't human, so won't matter none to him."

Greg motioned Lori to move back and took her place close to Marmalade. He held the cat firmly while Jim cleaned and bandaged the wound. Marmalade growled and squirmed, but

Jim completed the job quickly and stood back.

"Best I can do. Should change that dressing in a couple days."

"You charge extra for house calls?" Greg tried to sound relaxed, but his voice came out tight and betrayed his feelings.

Lori longed to do something to help. "May I give him some milk?"

Greg looked up. "You can try."

Lori went to get what had become Marmalade's bowl. Jim stood back and watched while she coaxed the cat to drink. He started toward the door until Greg called, "Wait up, Jim. I'll take this beggar home and make us some coffee. Don't know about you, but I need something after this. I'm no medic."

Lori gently petted Marmalade, who lay back against her hand after drinking some milk.

"Never knew that cat to let anyone near him 'cept you."

"The old tom's been sweet-talking Lori into giving him attention when I'm gone. Looks like he tried to bring her a fox fur."

Jim laughed. "I'll tell Mac to bring that fox tail by. Marmalade may want it as a trophy."

Greg picked up the cat. "Thanks, Lori. Sorry he messed up your quilt."

"It will wash." She stood barefoot, her long wet hair loose down her back. Greg's eyes held a new light as he looked at her.

"She's tamed more than the cat," Jim muttered.

"What say?" Greg turned away from Lori.

"Nothin'."

"Come on, then. Lori, will you join us?"

"No thanks." She suddenly realized how she looked and embarrassment filled her. What would Jim think to see Greg so at ease in her bedroom while she stood half-dressed and disheveled? "I'll come see Marmalade tomorrow."

The men left and Lori's trailer seemed empty. The silence closed in on her like a tangible thing. She pushed back the feeling and busied herself with mundane things. The quilt had to be washed, the berries she'd brought home had to be packaged and frozen, and the cranberry jelly put away.

She kept occupied, but time seemed to move like a snail. At eight o'clock, she carried her Bible and storybooks to the living room to prepare Sunday school lessons for the next morning.

A soft knock echoed in the silent house. She hastened to open the door. Greg stood holding a plate of sandwiches. "Have you eaten?"

"Guess I forgot." She held the door for him. "How's Marmalade?"

"Sleeping. He has a blanket next to my bed where he always sleeps. Maybe I should say usually sleeps." He put the plate on her coffee table. "Got any coffee?"

"How about hot chocolate?"

"Sounds good." He followed her to the kitchen and watched while she put milk to heat and took mugs down from the shelf.

"I feel responsible. I'm the one who let him out."

"Don't feel that way. He's tangled with a fox before. That time he got a chewed ear before he got loose. He's a tough guy. He'll survive."

They carried the mugs to the living room. Greg sat in the big chair and Lori curled her feet under her on the couch. "Sandwiches taste good. I never did fix supper."

Greg saw the books and papers scattered on the couch and floor. "Did I interrupt you?"

"I'm about finished." She picked up her Bible. "I was selecting verses to go with the story. I'll have the kids memorize them."

"And that's good?"

"Doesn't hurt. You ever read this?" She held up the Bible.

"Kalissa gave me one when I went to college."

"You read it?"

He squirmed a bit. "Not much."

"You should give it a try."

"Too many begets. I didn't like it."

"Try reading the Book of Acts or the Epistles of St. Paul.

No begets there. Only words to live by."

"I've gotten along without so far."

Lori smiled. "No harm in reading."

He took a bite of sandwich and didn't answer. When he'd finished the last bite, he asked, "Were you serious about cookies?"

She'd been picking up her papers and books, neatly stacking them on an end table. "Forgot about them." She jumped up and came back with the cookie jar. "Want some more cocoa?"

He handed her his empty cup and bit into a cookie. "Hey, these are good."

"Are you surprised?" she called from the kitchen.

His deep laugh echoed in the small room. "I deserve that. Say, I forgot your present. Be right back."

By the time she'd fixed more cocoa, he was back. He bounded back into her kitchen with such exuberance, she almost spilled the cocoa she was pouring.

"Guess what?" He held a package behind his back.

"Another loaf of bread?"

"Not quite." He held a package toward her with a big grin.

"A book." Lori took the present.

"You have to promise to practice on me."

She tore the paper open and held up a cookbook. "You really think I need this?" she quipped.

"Maybe not if all your cookies are this good." He grabbed another as he set their mugs down in the living room.

He munched cookies and talked about the day's hunting until it was time to leave. Lori followed him to the back door. He took her chin in his hand and tipped her head back. Giving her a kiss on the forehead, he remarked, "Oh, if the weather's good, I'm going to run my boat over to Uzinkie tomorrow. Would you check on Marmalade?"

Lori nodded her head. Would she ever understand this man? "Thanks for the cookbook," she said softly as he went down the steps.

❧

Lori's mood brightened the next morning when the little ones marched in at nine. She spent an hour reading to them and playing a guessing game. At ten, four of the older children came by. They helped her bake more cookies and talked about what their lives had been like before they moved to Monk's Island. Lori encouraged them to think about what it would be like to move back to the outside.

It was noon before she went to check on Marmalade. She found the cat on his blanket beside Greg's bed. The animal raised his head and offered a soft meow. Lori held the bowl of warm milk while the cat managed to lap up a little.

"You've got to eat, old man, or you won't get your strength back."

Marmalade settled back down and she stroked his head and back. She used a very gentle touch, as there were scabs in several places on his back. She left the milk and started back out.

Greg's house appeared neat and orderly. His bed was made and covered with a brown and red plaid spread. She looked closely at the pictures on his dresser. They appeared to be snapshots blown up and showing a village. Lori assumed the one of an older native woman was Kalissa. "Wow." Lori picked up the picture of the lovely young native girl. "Wonder who she is?" *Better stop snooping,* she told herself.

Lori checked on Marmalade a couple more times before she set off for Theresa's to baby-sit. She thought the cat's eyes didn't seem so glassy and he acted stronger.

Arriving at the noisy, cluttered trailer of the O'Briens' sent her spirits rising.

"Heard you found a cat in your bed. You using catnip flavored perfume?" Dennis teased.

Lori's laughter was forced. "Old Marmalade came in my place by mistake."

The children swarmed over her before Dennis could say more.

"Sure you're up to this?" Theresa asked.

"I had a total of nine this morning. Last time I counted, you only had four."

"Everyone is fed. Katie's night diaper and sleepers are on her crib. . ." Theresa rambled on with instructions.

"They'll be fine. Go along and have a good time."

Peggy clung to Lori's side, waiting for a chance to speak. "Did you really find a kitty?"

Lori bent down to the child, "No, it was Greg's cat. He got hurt and my door was open, so he crawled onto my bed."

"Is he okay now?"

"I just checked on him. He seemed a lot better and he drank some warm milk."

Dennis looked puzzled. "I thought I saw Greg's boat go out this morning. He go fishing?"

"Said he planned to go to Uzinkie. He asked me to look after Marmalade."

"He goes there a lot. Rumor is he's got a girlfriend there."

The picture of the beautiful young woman flashed through Lori's mind, sending a piercing pain racing down her spine. "He said he goes to see the lady who raised him," she offered weakly.

For once her spirits did not rise when she entertained the children. After stories and games, she bathed the boys and put them to bed. Next, she managed to get a wiggling Katie into sleepers and rocked her to sleep while she read to Peggy. By the time Dennis and Theresa came in at eleven, she felt tired and had a bit of a headache.

"Stay awhile and I'll make some tea," Theresa urged.

"Thanks, but I have to be up early for school. I'll take a rain check."

Both Dennis and Theresa thanked her profusely. As good friends as they were, Lori couldn't wait to get away.

At home, alone and in silence, she could no longer hold back the black gloom that invaded her thoughts. The picture of the lovely young woman haunted her. *Why do I care?* she kept asking herself. She didn't dare answer.

You know you could never love a man who doesn't share your faith, she scolded herself. Still the tears came. Lori cried herself to sleep.

seven

School and the children filled Lori's hours. Still she found she couldn't look at Greg without remembering the picture of the native girl. *Why am I tormenting myself?* she asked her mind over and over. *He isn't the one for me, so why do I care who his friends are?*

If Greg sensed any change in her attitude, he said nothing. Their friendship continued. He often brought her gifts of game or fish, and they spent many evenings together. Sometimes he would ask her questions about her work with the children. More often, they talked about his job or latest hunting or fishing trip.

Marmalade now hobbled around on three legs. His disability slowed the cat down considerably. Still, he managed to climb onto Lori's davenport and curl up next to her almost every night.

"How long are you going to keep him bandaged?" Lori asked Greg.

"Till that gash is well healed. He'll have a bad scar, but I think he'll be able to walk on it again."

The yellow striped animal stretched out next to Lori. He licked her hand as if trying to groom her the way he groomed himself.

"I can't get over how he's taken to you. I've had him five years and you're the first person he's ever made friends with."

"What's that in cat years? Maybe he's getting senile."

Greg smiled, lighting up his face in a way that twisted Lori's heart. "Old Marmalade is in his prime and showing good taste."

Lori only looked at Greg. Her heart betrayed her feelings while her mind kept reminding her they could only be friends. He's not a believer, her conscience screamed again and again.

84

She gathered her warring thoughts and tucked them into a back corner of her mind. Changing the subject, she asked, "Have you talked to Scott?"

"I think you're worried for nothing. He's quiet because his mind is busy. I've talked to a friend at the NOAA lab in Kodiak and he'll take Scott on a tour."

"What's Noah?" Her tone expressed her puzzlement.

"National Oceanic and Atmospheric Association. They do studies of marine life, fish counts, census of the different species, things like that."

"How interesting. Scott will be delighted with a treat like that." Excitement for her student filled Lori.

"Kid reads a lot. Orders books from the state library. He won't have trouble getting college scholarships."

Lori frowned. "It's college I worry about. He's lived so free here. Can he adapt to school, social life, things he's never experienced?"

"Sure he can." Greg grinned. "Scott spends a lot of time around the bunkhouse. He knows more about life than you give him credit for."

"I appreciate your taking an interest in him. Now if I can get you to talk to the rest of the kids about native ways."

His expression turned vacant. He stared at nothing. "No one wants to hear what I have to say."

"Why not?" Lori's anger reflected in her tone of voice.

Greg put his hands together and rubbed his beard. When he spoke, his thoughts came from a distance. His voice was soft, just above a whisper. "The natives build a village, but the whites hold the permanent jobs." He looked at her as he went on. "Like teachers, police, postmasters. The natives build the town, but they have no jobs to support it. They're trapped in a vicious circle. They used to be self-supporting. They lived off the land only a few years ago. Then they didn't need money. Now heating oil is flown in, electricity is fifty-four cents a kilowatt-hour, and water is nine cents a gallon. Too many of them can't cope—so they turn to alcohol." Greg's smile looked more like a grimace. "And too many whites judge all natives by the drunks they see sleeping in the street."

"Does it have to be that way? Don't some learn trades and professions?"

He shrugged. "Not enough. The majority are fatalistic. . .at the mercy of hurting events like they once were at the mercy of storms and animal migrations."

"Aren't you being fatalistic, too? You're quick to point out the bad parts. Aren't there any good things? Isn't life more than survival of the fittest now?"

Greg let his hands bang on the arms of his chair. "We need more Pollyannas like you. Yes, there's good. Medicine and care. Not everyone comes up here to make a fortune and leave. Not all agencies are arrogant. Good companies are setting up businesses where the natives can find work. It's a long road, though, from survival in a wild environment to survival in the twentieth century." He leaned back in the chair. "What got me started preaching? Sorry to bore you with my pet peeves."

Lori sat with her feet curled under her. Marmalade snuggled close by. "I know the problems are many. You wouldn't talk about them the way you do if you didn't feel strongly about it. It isn't the problems I want the children to hear about. I'd like them to know the history first. They need to know what survival in the environment meant in the past. Once they learn about the past, they will be able to understand the present and maybe help form the future."

Greg sat forward in his chair. "I have an idea. Would you exchange students with a friend of mine?"

"What do you mean?"

"I could ask the teacher in Kalissa's village to come talk to your students and you could go talk to hers." His eyes sparkled. His voice held enthusiasm.

"I. . .I think it's a good idea." In her mind Lori heard Dennis saying, *He's got a girlfriend.* Could this be the girl? "Where's the teacher from?"

"She grew up in the same village I did. She went to college at Fairbanks and came back to teach."

Lori felt as if a cold wind blew through her heart. He grew up with her. Now I know I don't stand a chance. She forced herself to speak. "I thought you said natives didn't get teaching jobs." She tried to keep her voice light, but her attempt at humor fell flat.

"Fortunately not all the young people who leave the village fail to come back."

"I hope if I leave this village, I won't fail to come back."

"I'll take you across in my boat. If you think that's bad, you should make the trip in a Bidarka."

"Is that one of those kayaks?"

"The Aleuts call them Bidarkas. They're a boat made of skins."

"You fix it up with your friend and I'll be glad to trade classes." One of her feet had gone to sleep, and she shifted her legs. Marmalade yowled in protest. "Oh! Poor baby, did I hurt you?" She slipped her hand under the cat, gently rubbing his hurt paw.

Greg's deep laugh filled the air. "You've got him so spoiled he isn't fit to live with. He's started to put weight on that leg again, so I doubt you hurt more than his pride. He likes your undivided attention."

"I'll go warm him some milk."

"He's always hated milk. He only drinks it to please you."

"Is that why you eat my cookies?"

Greg brushed the crumbs off his shirt. "I have to keep checking on your progress as a cook." He took another cookie from the jar at his side. "You sure this isn't leftover play dough?"

"No, honest, I used fresh peanut butter. Want something to wash the cookies down with?"

"Got any cold milk?"

"Sure." She brought Marmalade his saucer of warm milk and went to get Greg a glass of milk.

"Thanks. Did you try the Boleek Kalissa sent you?"

"It tastes like the salmon Dennis smoked."

Greg took another cookie. "That's what Boleek is. I gave

Dennis her recipe for brine. He'd be real proud if you told him his smoked salmon was as good as hers."

"I like the salmon, but the jerky he makes tastes like old shoes."

Greg's laugh filled her with a warm glow. She looked forward to the evenings they spent together. She treasured their friendship even when Greg's stoic indifference left her feeling rejected, frustrated, and alone. The weekends he spent away were her worst times. She filled them with parties for the children, but all the while she entertained and taught them, she stored away stories of things they said and did to share with him when he returned.

&

Greg took Scott with him the next time he went to Kodiak for a week. The boy had shouted "All right!" when Lori told him about the proposed trip to the NOAA lab. Betty and Bill had echoed their pleasure. "Appreciate your interest in our boy," Bill told her as he shyly offered her a package of frozen halibut.

"Greg set the trip up," she reminded Bill.

"Not without your prodding," Betty said in spite of the warning look from her husband. "Oh, I know, Bill, Greg's the authority around here, but Lori's made a difference in his attitude."

"He's lonesome, like the general who won't mix with the troops." Lori tried to smooth the situation.

She thought about the conversation now as she walked toward Theresa's. It was that time of year when she found it important to let school out at 2:30. The children needed time to enjoy a little daylight. It stayed dark until nine in the morning and dusk moved in at four in the afternoon. Evenings stretched long and lonely. Even with Marmalade's friendly purr, Lori's mood often matched the gloom outside.

Rather than face her empty home, she knocked on Theresa's door.

"Hi. Come on in. You may have saved my sanity," Theresa greeted her.

As she slid out of her shoes, Lori asked, "What's the problem?"

"Bad case of kid-i-tis."

"What?"

Theresa waved at her messy house. Toys lay scattered all over the floor and unfolded laundry draped every kitchen chair and the table. "I'm close to screaming in frustration." She plugged in the coffee pot.

Mark and Aaron raced up and down the hall. "Hey guys, it's not raining. Why don't you go out while it's still light? Come here and I'll help with your coats," Lori called to the rambunctious boys.

Theresa sighed, dumped unfolded diapers out of a chair, and plopped down. "I've been trying to get Aaron out all day, but Katie has done nothing but fuss. She won't take a nap and he's full of energy."

"Wish I could keep Mark longer, but a half-day is all the five-year-olds can handle of school."

"Don't know how you manage that much. He and Wayne Larsen together would finish me off."

Lori zipped Aaron's coat. "They know if they don't mind me they have to sit in the corner. Sitting still for fifteen minutes is torture."

Theresa got up to pour coffee. She grinned. "Didn't know you went in for child abuse."

With a final tug on Mark's hat, Lori shooed the boys out the back door and came back to drink her coffee. Between sips she folded diapers. "With so little daylight, the kids can't get out to run their energy off."

"You're telling me." Theresa held the cranky Katie. "By January I'll be ready for the funny farm."

"You told me when you got to this point, the kids did something cute to make it all worthwhile."

"I said that? Told you, I'm going nuts."

"Where's Peggy?"

"She went home with Debbie today. Liz says it helps her if Debbie has a playmate. The two of them play dolls by the hour." Theresa cradled Katie, who had finally gone to sleep. "I'll go put her down."

Lori grabbed an empty box and tossed toys and blocks into it. By the time Theresa came back, the kitchen floor no longer presented an obstacle course.

"You don't have to do that."

"I need a little exercise, too."

"Enough. Sit down and talk to me. Real adult conversation and no 'Mommy, I want a cookie' stuff."

Lori giggled, "Oh, what do you want to solve first, world hunger or world peace?"

Now Theresa laughed. "You'll have to break me in on something easier than that, Teacher. What do you hear from home?"

"Priscilla writes faithfully. Scares me."

"Scares you? Whatever for?"

"The bazaars, sewing circles, and potlucks are starting to sound tempting."

Theresa grinned. "See, I told you so. You'll be counting the days until school's out and you can go home."

Lori put her cup down and stared at the brown liquid. "I don't want to go back." She looked up. "I don't know what I want."

"Greg?" Theresa's teasing tone brought a blush to Lori's face.

A chilling scream rent the air, sending goose bumps over Lori's arms. Both women jumped. Theresa raced for the door with Lori only a step behind. Neither woman stopped for shoes. They plunged down the steps in the direction of the blood-curdling sound.

Theresa stopped so suddenly, Lori bumped into her. Both gasped. Theresa gave a strangled cry as she dropped to her knees beside the prostrate body of Aaron.

Lori looked at the scene as if she were disembodied. Separated from emotion, she saw the crumpled child with blood pouring over his face. A shovel lay close by. Mark stood frozen in horror, staring at his brother. She heard rather than saw someone vomiting by Sandy's back door. It seemed like slow motion, but it actually took Lori only seconds to respond.

The rocks cut her feet as she raced to the bunkhouse. Still holding her feelings at bay, she ran through the door yelling, "Jim, Jim!"

The grizzled old man stood up quickly, sending his chair sprawling. Mike came from the kitchen, wiping his hands on the apron covering his paunch. Panting for breath, Lori gasped, "Need a medic. Aaron's hurt."

Jim took her arm and tried to guide her to a chair.

"No time to lose. He's bleeding bad and he's unconscious."

"Is he crying?"

"No."

Jim went into action. "Mike, get on the radio to the Coast Guard. Get them here fast." He grabbed his black box. "Where's the boy, Missy?"

Lori took a deep breath. "By the O'Briens' trailer."

"Get in the truck. We's as good as there."

The truck skidded to a stop. Theresa still knelt by Aaron's body. She vainly tried to staunch the flow of blood with a wet towel. More people stood watching, their faces registering horror. Lori looked for Mark, but before she could seek him out, Jim commanded, "Get a glass of water. Don't look like I can do much for the boy. Best calm his mama down."

Lori fought to keep her emotions from screaming out of control. *Can't do much for the boy. Dear God, what did he mean?* She stumbled into the O'Briens' trailer for a glass of water. On her way out, she glanced in the crib to find Katie still sound asleep.

Walking toward Theresa, balancing the glass of water, Lori heard Jim say, "Head wound always looks bad. Lot of blood."

"But he's unconscious," Theresa whispered.

"Got a chopper comin'. He's goin' to be okay." Jim took the glass from Lori's shaking hand and handed Theresa a tablet. She tried to push it away.

"You need it. The medics don't need another patient to take care of." His gruff voice belied the concern showing in his face.

Theresa took the pill. She held the glass up to Lori. "Dennis . . .got to tell Den."

"Mike's on the radio, Miz O'Brien. Dennis'll be right in."

Hope he's right, Lori thought, as she looked around again for Mark. She saw Betty standing with her arm around Sandy. The young woman's sickly pallor reminded Lori of the earlier sound of someone retching. Seeing Jim tending to Aaron and Theresa, Lori walked toward the two women.

Sandy's whole body shook. Her deathly white face registered shock. "I saw it. . .I saw it," she gasped over and over.

Lori looked at Betty and took Sandy's hand. "Saw what? Tell us what happened."

"They were playing." Her eyes glazed as if seeing the boys as they were. "Told me they were going to dig a pit for bears." A new series of shudders ran over Sandy's body, and Lori saw Betty draw the woman even closer.

"It's going to be all right, Sandy. Just tell us what you saw."

"Mark. . .Mark picked up the big shovel." She leaned forward gagging. Betty held her and Lori patted her, speaking in a soft, reassuring voice.

"Was it the shovel?"

"Yes. . .it's so heavy, and Mark tried to hold it over his head. He staggered and it dropped on Aaron's. . ." Her voice ended in a moan.

Betty looked up from Sandy. "Blade must have gone in. Has he come to yet?"

"No, Mike's called the Coast Guard."

Looking at the failing light, Betty muttered, "Hope they can make it."

Fear too strong to blot out squeezed Lori's heart. "What if. . ." she mouthed inaudibly.

"Barge takes hours."

Her squeezed heart landed in her stomach, causing a dangerous churning. Lori swallowed the bile and turned to watch over the boy with the rest of the quiet group. A truck roared over the rough road, breaking the silence.

Dennis leaped from the vehicle to his wife's side in one

bound. "What happened?" He took in the pale crumbled body of his son. The child's head lay wrapped in a bloody towel. He dropped on his knees by Aaron.

Jim spoke, but Lori didn't think Dennis heard anything. "Got hit with a shovel. Bled a lot. Might be a fracture, so didn't move him until medics get here."

Dennis looked up. The overcast sky had already took on the hew of dusk. "They can't come in now." His voice shook with the terror showing in his vivid blue eyes. He turned his gaze to Lori. "How did it happen?" he demanded.

"The boys were playing. The big shovel's so heavy, Mark lost control of it and Aaron got in the way."

Dennis lunged to his feet. "Mark. . .where's Mark?" he bellowed.

"No, Dennis, no. It's not Mark's fault." Lori grabbed his arm.

He shook her off as if she were no more than a fly. "Mark, where are you?"

Shorty arrived from the bunkhouse. "Saw him down by the water a minute ago."

Dennis pushed people back in his race to the shore. Lori hastened to catch up to the big man. This time she felt the sharp stones on her feet as she struggled to hurry. She stopped short when she saw the small figure huddled where the waves washed over his feet. Lori felt her tears run unrestrained as the overwrought father scooped the little boy into his bear-like arms and sobbed openly.

"It's going to be all right, Son."

Creeping closer, Lori could hear the plaintive little voice. "I killed him." The small body rocked back and forth in his father's arms. "Daddy. . .Daddy, I didn't mean to."

Dennis rubbed his tear-streaked face against Mark's curly hair. "I know, I know. Aaron will be okay."

Mark tried to pull away. "I can walk in the water and go away."

Lori choked back a sob. She longed to go to the father and son, but she knew she must not intrude.

"No, Son, you can't leave us. We love you too much. We have to go back to Mommy now." He and Lori looked up as the first sounds of the approaching helicopter reached them.

Within moments the aircraft had landed and two medics bent over Aaron. Theresa stood close to Dennis, who still cradled Mark in his arms. Peggy clung to her mother's side.

The young Coast Guard medic looked at the huddled family group. "He's got a nasty cut and a probable fracture. Going to have to take him to the hospital for a few days."

Lori saw the look that passed between Theresa and Dennis. "You go with Aaron," Lori said. "I'll take care of the girls and Mark."

Betty and Liz spoke at once. "Lori's right. You go with your boy. We'll help her with the kids."

"Make it fast. Be dark soon," the pilot yelled from the beach.

The medic carefully picked Aaron up, explaining, "He's too small for a stretcher." Blindly, Theresa followed him.

Dennis looked from Aaron to Mark. "I love you, boy," he whispered to the small head against his chest. "Got to go with Mommy. Will you be okay now?"

Lori thought she would never again see such pain as Mark's eyes held. He nodded almost imperceptibly as Dennis lowered him to the ground. Quickly, she knelt between Peggy and Mark, hugging them to her.

"Hal'll be in tomorrow. We'll send some clothes to you and Theresa," Betty called to Dennis as he jogged toward the waiting helicopter.

The rest of the men were coming in now and wives turned to go home. Subdued talk hummed as the helicopter faded into the darkening sky.

Lori coaxed the children back in the house. Katie's chatter greeted them as they went through the back door.

"Can you get your coats hung up while I see what Katie wants?"

Peggy took Mark's hand and led him toward the kitchen.

Neither of them stopped to take their shoes off. Lori noted the muddy tracks left by Mark.

"Peggy, could you help Mark take off his wet shoes and socks. His feet must be cold."

"Yes, Mom. . .I mean, Miss Wilson."

Sighing deeply, Lori plunged into the tasks at hand. Katie had to be changed. Then Mark needed to be cajoled out of his wet overalls, shoes, and socks. Peggy helped her find pajamas for him. Lori felt the little girl's eyes watching her as she prepared to feed Katie. Mark remained in the big chair in the living room where she'd put him while she changed his clothes. He stared into space. "He looks catatonic," Lori said under her breath.

"Is Mark sick, too?" Peggy asked timidly while Lori spooned baby food into Katie's waiting mouth.

"He's scared. We'll have to give him lots of love for a few days." She paused to hug Peggy to her side. "You're my big helper." Katie pounded on her high chair tray, demanding more applesauce.

Feeling pulled in three different directions, Lori gave Katie a cracker and went to rinse out the baby food jar. She had started to open a can of soup for Peggy and Mark, when a knock at the door interrupted her. Betty came in without waiting for an invitation.

"How you doing? Need some help?"

Lori turned in relief at the sound of another adult. "I don't know how Theresa does it."

"For one thing, she only had one at a time. Taking on three at once can be intimidating."

"Oh." Lori grabbed the pan as the soup boiled over. "Thought I could feed Mark some of this."

"How's he doing?"

Lori shrugged and pointed to the pathetic figure. "What should I do?"

"Try the soup." Betty picked up a toy and put it within Katie's reach. "Sit up here, Peggy, and tell me about the dolls you and Debbie have while you eat some supper."

Grateful for the help, Lori turned her attention to Mark. She picked him up and carried him to the kitchen. Holding him in her lap, she spooned soup into him much the same way she'd fed Katie applesauce. His head lay against her breast, making it difficult not to spill the hot liquid.

"Are you warm now, Mark?"

He looked up, his blue eyes, so like his father's, luminous in his white face. "Where's Daddy?"

"He and Mommy took Aaron to the hospital."

"Aaron's dead." His soft voice echoed with agony.

"No, Mark. Aaron got a cut on his head, but he'll be all right."

"He didn't talk to me."

"He kind of went to sleep. People do that sometimes when they get hurt. The doctor said Aaron will come home in a few days."

Peggy had ceased to talk about dolls. She listened to Lori. "Are you going to stay here?"

"Yes." Lori brushed back the dark curls, trying to reassure the little girl.

"But you have to go to school."

Betty patted Peggy's shoulder. "There are lots of us who will help. I'll come back in the morning to take care of Katie."

Betty washed dishes and picked up the rest of the scattered toys, while Lori read to Peggy and Mark. The children cuddled close to her on the couch. Katie sat looking at her cloth books while Lori read. Exhausted by his shattering experience, Mark fell asleep.

Lori laid him in his bed. With Betty's help, the other two were soon tucked in as well.

"Could you stay a minute while I run home and get some clean clothes and feed Marmalade?"

"That cat moved in with you now?"

"Only when Greg's gone."

❧

Lori slept fitfully on the O'Briens' couch. Mark cried out a couple times and she soothed him back to sleep. The next day started early when Katie started to cry at six a.m.

The baby wanted Mommy and would settle for nothing less. Lori tried rocking her, feeding her, playing with her, and finally put her on the floor to howl while she took care of Mark and Peggy. "I hope Katie isn't coming down with something," she muttered, remembering Theresa saying the baby had fussed the day before also.

When Betty arrived at quarter to eight, Lori felt she had been up for hours.

Mark still did not respond when she spoke to him. His pale face accented the dark smudges under his eyes. Peggy stirred her oatmeal around and around without taking a bite.

"Time to leave for school. Get your coats and I'll help you put them on." The threesome trudged off to the little red schoolhouse.

The undercurrent in the classroom set off sparks. "You get a whipping?" Wayne demanded of Mark, who appeared to shrink another two inches into his sweater collar.

"Come to order, class." Lori's voice commanded respect. "As you know, Aaron O'Brien had an accident yesterday." She looked sternly at Wayne. "It was no one's fault. Aaron is in the hospital in Kodiak, and I ask that you be extra nice to his brother and sister. They feel bad just as you would be sad if someone you loved got hurt." She watched Mark while she spoke. He sat staring vacantly. *I don't think he heard a word I said,* she told herself.

"Now it's time to get on with lessons." Assignments were given and homework corrected. Time crept forward as the students settled down to the tasks at hand. At eleven o'clock, Liz came by to pick up Mark and Peggy for lunch.

"Did you bring a sandwich?" Liz asked Lori.

"Forgot in all the rush."

Liz smiled. "I thought you might." She pulled a brown paper bag from behind her back and handed it to Lori. "Bribery. Can Debbie and Peggy have the rest of the day off?"

"Sure," Lori answered, puzzled by the request.

"Dolls need a tea party," Liz said, loud enough for the girls to hear. Quietly she added, "And Mark needs companions."

"Thanks." Lori patted her friend's arm.

After lunch break, Lori concentrated on helping Pete with a math problem and only glanced up when she heard a plane come in. After the longest day she'd ever lived, she checked her watch and saw it was 2:30. Before she could excuse her students, Greg strode into the room.

The children started to chatter. Greg raised his hand for silence. Glancing at Lori, he announced, "I've been to the hospital. Aaron is going to be fine." He paused for the cheer that went up and then continued, "He's going to have quite a scar on his forehead and right now he has a fractured skull. Okay, you can go home now and share the news with your folks."

Lori sank into her chair.

"You look beat."

"I am. Now I have to go pick up Katie, do laundry, and fix supper."

"Theresa said you were staying with the kids. Can I help?"

Lori looked up, trying not to let her feelings show. A sigh escaped before she could snatch it back.

Greg put his big hand over hers. "Got to check with Whitney and then I'll be over." He started to leave, turning back as he got to the door. "Are we having meat loaf for supper?"

It seemed a month ago rather than only the day before that Lori had walked to the O'Briens' from school. Today she found Katie jabbering in her swing, the house looked neat, and Betty stood at the kitchen table folding diapers.

"Think the baby's teething." Betty pointed to Katie, who chewed on a rubber ring. "Stick that in the freezer and give it to her real cold when she gets fussy."

"I'll never make it as a mother," Lori groaned.

"Sure you will. It comes naturally."

Lori sat down heavily and took the coffee Betty offered. "I've got a lot more respect for a mother's job."

Heading for the bedroom to put the stack of clean clothes

away, Betty said, "You get into a routine and that helps."

"Scott get back okay?"

"Yes. I'm anxious to hear all about it. You going to be okay here now?"

"Sure. Thanks for everything. You go enjoy your family now that you've got this one organized."

Peggy and Mark came home from Liz's. Peggy chattered about dolls and tea parties. Mark went back to the big chair and sat staring at nothing. Lori made up a story to amuse them as she went about preparing supper. Peggy helped her find things. Mark offered nothing.

At five when Greg walked in, Peggy sat on the living room floor coloring. Katie shook the side of her crib to announce she had finished her nap. Mark sat with the unopened book still in his lap. At the sound of a man's voice, Mark's eyes brightened. The light faded when it wasn't Dennis who came through the door. Greg walked directly to the boy and swung him in the air. "How's my fishing buddy?" Playing with the children, he casually talked about their brother. "He's got a big white bandage on his head. He looks like a pirate. Oh, Mark, he wants to know if you got a bear in the pit yet."

Mark looked stricken, then flinging himself at Greg, the little boy started to cry. Great sobs racked his body. Greg held him and motioned Lori to stay back.

Lori put Katie on the floor and she quickly crawled to the crayons. Peggy snatched a crayon away from the baby, whose howls of anger joined her brother's sobs of relief.

Lori looked from one to the other in dismay. Clamping her mouth in a straight line, the teacher in her spoke up. "Peggy, please pick up the crayons. Miss Kate, time for you to eat." She put the baby in her high chair, handed her a cracker, and proceeded to set the table for supper. She watched in wonder as Greg continued to bring Mark back to reality.

Her happiness glowed when they sat down together and Greg asked the blessing without being prompted. Her cup of happiness ran over when Mark said, "This meat loaf tastes like Mommy's."

eight

Fog blanketed the island. No plane could penetrate the murk that enveloped Monk's. Dennis could not fly home but he did keep in contact. Each day he reported Aaron's progress to K.A.T.'s Kodiak office. They sent radio bulletins to all the anxious friends waiting in the logging camp. Greg used the radio in his trailer to relay Lori's message to the O'Briens, assuring them the rest of the children were fine.

The second day after the accident, Greg arrived at school to take Mark home. "Got important business with my fishing buddy," he told Lori in front of the assembled students.

Grateful to see Mark's much improved demeanor, Lori hugged the boy and sent him off with Greg.

That afternoon Lori found the O'Brien trailer clean and Katie taking a nap. "This place looks great," she exclaimed, expecting to see Betty. Instead Greg greeted her.

"Got coffee perking," he offered, getting up from where he and Mark had been playing a game on the living room floor.

Mark ran to tackle her by the knees. "Teacher, Teacher, I talked to my daddy."

Lori looked up from where she had knelt to hug the boy. Greg's grin lit his face and made his blue eyes dance. "Told you we had business to take care of."

"I talked on the radio," Mark told her.

"Had my office in Kodiak phone the O'Briens and then patch that call to my CB. Theresa sends her thanks and says Aaron is progressing all right."

"Where are they staying?"

Greg looked surprised. "I thought you arranged it."

She shook her head. "You're talking in riddles."

"Theresa said your friend Joe Nesbitt invited them to stay with him."

100

It took a moment, but then she exclaimed, "I remember now. He sat next to me on the flight from Anchorage to Kodiak last summer. Said he was in the Coast Guard."

"You sure made some first impression. Theresa made it sound like you were old buddies."

"I'm glad they have a place to stay." She stooped to pick up a crayon Peggy had missed when she'd picked up. Katie would think it delicious. "It could have cost Dennis a fortune to stay in a motel."

"He'd like to get back to work. He'll be back as soon as a plane can get in. Theresa will stay until Aaron can come home."

"How long will that be?" Lori filled coffee cups before she sat down.

"Getting tired of being a substitute mommy?"

She scowled in mock anger. "Of course not. Just thinking of the kids. They miss her a lot."

He chuckled as angry shouts issued from the children's bedroom, where Mark had gone to play with Peggy. "Sounds like normal to me." The din woke Katie, whose howls added to the noise. Greg got up, motioning Lori to stay put. "I'll take them up to my place for a while. Bread dough must be ready and we can bake some for supper."

"Inviting yourself for supper again?"

He looked hurt.

Hastily she added, "Just joking. You know I'd do anything for homemade bread."

"Remind me never to teach you to bake your own."

She sighed in contentment as she followed him to the children's room. She whisked Katie out of her crib onto her hip and watched Greg as he helped Mark and Peggy with their jackets. *He seems so comfortable with children*, she thought. She blushed in confusion when he turned around and reached out to her. When it was Katie he bent to kiss, she attempted to hide her feelings.

When Greg and the older children left, Katie sat in the middle of the living room, trying to pile one block on another. Lori curled up with papers she needed to grade.

"Anybody home?"

"Come on in." Lori stacked her books and papers out of Katie's reach and headed for the door.

"How come it's so quiet?" Sandy asked, coming down the hall from the wanagan.

"Simple. I put a kid in each corner and stand in the middle of the room with a whip."

Sandy's smile didn't reach her eyes. "I'm sorry I haven't been over to help."

"Are you feeling better?"

"No." The pale young woman plopped heavily in the living room chair.

Concern wiped the smile from Lori's face. "What is it? Do you have a cold?"

Sandy looked up, her eyes wide and imploring. "I could have prevented it," she whispered.

Lori knelt on the floor by Katie. She shook her head. "Sandy, it was an accident."

As if she hadn't heard, the listless woman continued. "He said he was going to dig a pit. I should have asked how or where or something."

Lori reached up and took Sandy's cold hand in hers. "I'm at fault, not you. I sent the boys out to play."

Sandy's blond hair flipped back and forth as she shook her head. "No, no."

"See, it really was an accident." Gently, Lori squeezed Sandy's hand.

A flicker of hope showed in the white face. "You believe that?"

"Of course. We can't change what happened and you shouldn't torment yourself by trying. How could any of us know Mark would drop the shovel or that Aaron would be in the way?"

Sandy pulled her hand free to brush back her hair. She laughed as Katie's blocks fell over again and the baby picked one up and threw it. "She's got a bit of a temper." The laugh turned into a deep sigh. "Thanks, Lori. I dreaded coming here, but I had to face it. I didn't think I'd ever be able to look Theresa in the eyes again. Are you sure she won't blame me?"

"Why would she? We all know you love the kids and wouldn't hurt them." Katie tired of the blocks and grabbed onto Lori's sweater. "Okay, okay, I'll pay attention to you." She swept the baby into the air. "Watch this." Lori stood Katie up to the coffee table, where the little girl alternately slapped her hands on the surface and tried to walk along the side of it.

More color filled Sandy's cheeks and her eyes sparkled as she watched the baby. "Wow, she'll be walking soon." She looked at Lori with a new glow in her face. "We're going to have a baby next year."

"Hey, that's great. When are you expecting?"

Sandy giggled. "I'm not, but I hope to get that way in Hawaii."

"When do you leave?"

"Steve will quit the end of November."

"Thanksgiving will be your going-away party."

"I'll be thankful to get off this island," she reached out to clasp Lori's hand, "but I'll miss the friends I have here."

❧

The papers were graded. Potatoes boiled on the stove and canned vegetables heated on a low heat. Salmon steaks sat in marinade ready to broil. Lori spooned carrots into Katie's open mouth and wondered, *Will I ever have a baby of my own?* Greg and the children burst through the back door, breaking up her reverie.

After dinner, as they washed dishes together, she asked, "Did you know Sandy and Steve are leaving the end of November?"

"Lots of guys pull out the first of December. Things slow down when the weather's bad. Whitney won't have a ship in to load logs until March or April."

"Will I lose kids out of school?"

"Don't know. Mostly it's single men who head for the sunshine. The married ones keep working."

"Why's that?"

He looked surprised at her question. "Single guys have money to blow. Married ones have responsibilities."

"Oh." *Maybe that's why Greg says he has no time for women,* her mind suggested. A loud thump followed by Mark's cry of pain sent her thoughts flying as she scurried to soothe the child's hurts. A cold cloth covered his bumped head as she held him and listened to his stories of playing at Greg's.

❧

It seemed like she just got the children settled down and fell asleep on the couch when Katie's cry heralded a new day. The mist persisted, but a brief break in the weather allowed Dennis to fly home that afternoon.

The sound of a plane and the promise of mail and groceries made it impossible to keep her students' attention. Lori dismissed them a half hour early and went to check with Dennis.

"Aaron's okay. The trip over was a rough one. Poor little guy came to before we got to Kodiak." Dennis grinned. "He threw up all over the medic taking care of him."

"Did Mommy get mad?" Peggy asked as she pressed close to her father's side.

"No, honey. We were too worried about Aaron to think about anything but getting him better and back home with you."

"When will Mommy come home?" Mark asked from where he stood in the circle of his father's arms.

"Real soon. Mommy just wants to stay in town until Aaron's stitches come out." Dennis turned to Lori. "Say, that friend of yours has sure been nice to us. He walks to work so Theresa can have his car to drive."

Lori felt her cheeks burn. "I only met him on the plane flying in from Anchorage."

"Good thing for us he remembered you."

Having their daddy home had Peggy, Mark, and Katie so wound up it took extra time to get them settled for the night. "You don't have to stay," Dennis told her.

"Be nice to get back to my own bed," Lori admitted. "I'll be back at six to get Peggy and Mark ready for school."

Her own trailer stood dark. The silence poured over her as she sank into the living room chair and heard only the rain dripping off the roof. *I'll never make a good mother. This is too blissful,* she told herself, giving up her anxieties of the past days to relax in the world she'd created within the walls of her trailer. She set her alarm for five and slipped gratefully into the first good night's rest she'd had since the accident.

When she arrived at the O'Briens' the next morning, all three children clamored for her immediate attention.

"Daddy burned the toast," Peggy complained. Mark cried because he couldn't find his other shoe. No one had time to figure out why Katie added her cry to the confusion.

"I'm going to go run a grader where it's quiet," Dennis yelled above the din.

Within ten minutes Katie chewed on a piece of burned toast, Peggy ate Cheerios, and Mark wore two shoes. "Any coffee left?" Lori asked.

Dennis stood in the middle of the kitchen shaking his head. "Don't know how she stands it. No wonder Theresa didn't want to come home for a few days." He poured Lori a mug of coffee. "Sure appreciate your taking over."

"Once you get in a routine, it's not bad. And," she admitted, "I've had a lot of help."

The day went smoothly. Dennis complimented her on the salmon loaf and ate the rest of Greg's homemade bread. The children settled down early, and Lori climbed the hill to her home feeling good.

"Well, hello, old man. I've missed you." Marmalade stood on his hind legs to push his head against her hand.

She and the cat barely had time to turn on the lights in her living room before Greg stuck his head in the back door, calling, "Anybody home?" He saw his cat rubbing against Lori's legs. "He missed you."

She reached down to pet the big tabby. "His foot looks all healed."

"Are you superstitious?"

"No, why?"

"First it was Marmalade, then Aaron, who's next?"

She shook her head. "I don't follow you."

His smile broke the usual stern set of his face. "Things happen in threes."

"Kalissa teach you that?"

"Maybe. Don't remember where it came from." He settled in his usual spot.

Lori started the tea kettle and turned on the radio. "First time I get to a store, I'm going to buy a tape player."

"KVOK getting to you?"

"Let's just say I don't like their taste in music."

"You planning a trip off island?"

"Thought maybe I could combine a trip to Kodiak with the visit to Uzinkie."

"Could work out." He took the cup of tea she offered him. "I'll see if we can get you on the next flight I charter for K.A.T."

"By the way, I don't think I properly thanked you for taking Scott. He talks of nothing else. He wants to work on a crab boat for NOAA next summer. Thinks he can be a lab tech."

"My friend at the lab mentioned it to him. The technicians tag and release the crab. Then when the crabbers find the tags in their pots, they return them so NOAA can chart the movements of the various kinds of crab."

"Doesn't excite me, but then, not everyone wants to teach school."

"Where will you teach next year?"

His question startled her. "Hadn't thought about it. Won't this school be here next year?"

"Whitney's contract is about filled. Hard to say what will happen. You'll be going back to New York, won't you?"

"Maybe," she answered vaguely. *What are you going to do?* her conscience taunted. Idly, she stroked Marmalade. "Where will you go?"

"Natives own forty-four million acres in Alaska. I'll find a place somewhere managing a part of it."

"Does K.A.T. manage all that?" Lori was impressed.

Greg laughed. "No. That's the land part of the Natives Claims Settlement Act of '71. There are many native corporations set up to manage their resources. I was just a kid when the Settlement Act was signed, and it's why I got a degree in forest management and came home to work. K.A.T. has a good record of management, and we hope to get more native corporations to join us."

"I hear so much about native Alaskans and I've yet to meet one." She put her hand up. "Okay, you were born here, so you're a native."

"No, I was born in Seattle. As soon as Theresa gets home, we'll get you to Uzinkie and complete your education."

"Take more than a couple days in a village. I'm still learning about this place and I've been here for months."

He stood and stretched. "You're doing great. Now let me take this beggar and go home." His beard brushed her face as he bent over and scooped up the protesting Marmalade. Lori swallowed and kept her eyes down so he couldn't look into them. *Why do I let him affect me so much?* she screamed within herself.

❧

Sleep did not come quickly. Lori scolded herself for reacting to Greg like some silly schoolgirl. Then she thought about his question of what she would do next year.

He's right, I've got to make a decision.

Troubled sleep did not bring the answers she sought.

❧

The stars sparkled brightly in the night sky when she made her way to the O'Briens' at six the next morning. By ten the sun shown brightly through the schoolhouse windows. All her students gazed out the windows and wiggled in their seats. It took skill and stern discipline to keep them at their lessons until 2:30.

As they fled the schoolhouse in a burst of energy, Lori heard the plane come in and hurried to the door to watch Hal land. As soon as she saw Theresa pop out the plane door, she grabbed her jacket and raced to the beach.

Mark spotted his mother and ran ahead of everyone yelling, "Mommy, Mommy." Lori caught up with Betty and Peggy, who were part of the greeting committee.

Theresa stood with Aaron in her arms, talking to Hal as he off-loaded cargo. Lori watched her turn with a smile of pleasure when Mark tackled her. The young mother put Aaron on his feet. The two boys stood still, staring at each other until Aaron put up his hands and growled.

"I'm a bear, rowwwer!"

Lori took Peggy's hand as they watched. Aaron wore a dark brown fake fur hat that had ears, eyes, and even a nose. With the hat pulled down over his ears, the bear's nose covered his scarred forehead. Mark squealed in delight and grabbed his brother.

"Then you get a bear hug."

The two little boys scuffled in the beach stones, patting and poking each other. Tears appeared in more than Lori's eyes as friends and neighbors watched the brothers' reunion.

"Need a ride Miz O'Brien?" Old Jim and his battered truck stood by the plane.

"Believe it or not, Jim, I missed this place. I want to walk and look at it and try to figure out why. Will you bring my stuff up?"

"Sure thing. The boy okay now?"

Theresa put out a hand to the grizzled man. "Thanks to you, Jim. You're always there when we need you."

He hung his head and tugged at his cap. "Weren't nothin'. Seen worse cuts in my day."

"I'll bet you have, but not on so small a logger. I'm so glad you were there to do the right thing when I was in such a panic."

His rheumy eyes sparkled. " 'Tweren't nothing, Miz O'Brien. I got to be getting this stuff delivered now." Spryly he headed for the boxes Hal handed down from the back of the plane.

Theresa turned back toward Lori. Peggy pulled free and ran to her mother, who stooped to give her daughter a hug and kiss. Betty tried her best to hold a screeching Katie. Theresa looked over Peggy's head and laughed. "What a welcome! It got so quiet at Joe's I had to come home." She stood up, took Peggy's hand, and reached out for Katie with her other arm.

"She's got a new tooth to show you," Betty said, relinquishing her hold on the baby.

Katie bounced and chattered while Theresa attempted to hear what Peggy tried to tell her. The boys alternately eyed each other and tentatively poked one another as if not believing the other was real.

"Let's go home," Theresa said. "Come on people, we'll have coffee and you can catch me up on the island gossip."

The children ran in and out the back door while the assembled women drank the coffee Lori made. They talked as if they hadn't seen each other in weeks.

Theresa sang the praises of Joe Nesbitt and knowing looks were exchanged in spite of Lori's protest. "I only met him once. He sat next to me on the plane from Anchorage."

"He's awfully nice," Theresa said again.

"He seemed nice when I talked to him but not enough for me to make a big deal about him. I am glad he gave you a place to stay, but I don't plan to go running into town to visit him."

The assembled women laughed and Liz teased, "You like the crop of bachelors on Monk's better? Come on, you can tell us. Is it George or Shorty you're holding out for?"

"After a week of my kids, she's probably a confirmed old maid."

Sandy's laugh turned to a look of chagrin. "Wish I could get pregnant as easy as you do, Theresa."

Talk turned from Lori to advice for Sandy. Gratefully, Lori peeked out back to check on the kids and went back to putting a casserole together for supper. The smell of food cooking reminded the wives they had husbands due home from work. Soon the party broke up.

"Can you manage now?" Lori asked her friend.

"I don't know what we'd have done without you." Theresa

put Katie in her high chair. "The house looks great, supper's cooking, and you still teach school. I'm impressed."

"Actually, I'm behind a little in lesson plans. Do you think I could sneak out early tonight?"

"Hey, you're not the maid. Stay for supper?"

Lori shook her head, but she was warmed with love as the kids trooped in and Aaron tugged on her sweater. "See my stitches." Lori picked the little boy up and exclaimed over the angry red scar on his forehead. "Makes you look very distinguished."

Aaron looked worried. "Is that good?"

"Very good, honey." Lori hugged and carried him to the living room, where she played with all the children "oohing" and "ahhing" in the right places while they told her about their games of the day and their dreams for tomorrow. Finally she got up. "All this is wonderful, guys, but I have work to do."

Theresa took her turn at giving Lori a hug. "Someday I'll make it up to you."

Lori shrugged in embarrassment. "I'm just thankful to have a friend like you." She hugged Theresa back. When she pulled back, she teased, "Besides, I like to have people indebted to me."

Leaving the hassle and howls behind, Lori started for home. "Mmmm, maybe I got some mail on the plane." The bunkhouse door stood open, so she walked over to the square boxes Jim had built on the wall and took two envelopes out of the one marked "Wilson."

Mike called "hi" from the kitchen, where the clatter of pans told her the men would find their dinner waiting when they came in from work.

"See you later, Mike." Her interest turned to the mail. A look at the return addresses told her the weekly letter from Priscilla had arrived. The second letter caused a twist in her chest and skip in her breathing. "Fred Potter," she read from the return address. A twinge of guilt tugged her. "I haven't thought about him in weeks," she muttered. Tucking the two letters in her pocket, she continued her walk home.

She drank in the clean air and marveled anew at the breath-taking view over the bay. A breeze played over the blue water, painting patterns with bits of white foam and breakers in the fading light. Two eagles hung in the air currents before resuming their lazy circle over the spruce-covered cliff that formed the bay. She sighed deeply, unable to equate the scene she looked at with anything she'd left in New York. What prompted Fred to write after all this time? What would he think of Monk's Island?

The evening called to her. Lori didn't want to go inside yet, so she walked out to her favorite log in front of her trailer and sat down. She watched the shadows spread across the sky. *Better read your mail,* part of her mind demanded.

Too dark, came the easy answer.

You afraid to face what's in the envelopes?

"Mmmm." Reluctantly, Lori rose and entered her trailer. A fresh loaf of bread waited on her kitchen table. A note in Greg's sprawling hand invited, "Come over later." The signature consisted of a crude drawing of a cat's paw print.

Lori put the note back on the table, tossed her jacket on the back of a chair after extracting the letters, and dropped into the big chair in the living room.

Fred's letter went on for pages and pages. He'd numbered each one and written in his precise handwriting. Lori read and reread what he'd written.

> . . .*I've been made assistant vice president at the bank. This makes it possible for me to offer you the life you deserve.* . .

Lori let the pages drop into her lap. Life I deserve. She stared unseeing into the darkened sky outside and wondered, *What do I deserve?*

Fred's letter went on to describe his work, his pay, his plans, all in great detail. ". . .Mother is past seventy and won't be with us much longer. I'd like you to keep the house as it is for now. Later you can redo it however you please. . ."

Wonder if he has her funeral planned, too.

Don't be crude, her conscience scolded.

In spite of herself, Lori thought of the beautiful old two-

story white house that would be Fred's. Her mind quickly
pulled down the heavy drapes and tossed out the worn, overstuffed furniture.

Shame on you, her mind cried. *You're as bad as he is, making plans for when his poor old mother dies.*

Lori closed her eyes and tears slipped through her lashes.
*Am I a fool or what? Chasing rainbows in a romantic dream.
Fred offers security, wife of the bank president, tea on Thursday afternoon, church on Sunday.* The pages fluttered to the
floor. *And he's a good Christian.*

What do you want? The taunt echoed painfully in her mind.

With a deep sigh, Lori tried to shake away the gloom by
tearing open the letter from Priscilla. She had learned to
respect Priscilla in the months away from New York. The past
few days in Theresa's home had reinforced what Lori now
knew to be true. Moving into another woman's house, even
one without a spoiled younger sister-in-law, could be a trial.
Now Fred offered her his mother's house. Could she do as
well as Priscilla had?

News of friends from school nudged a bit of nostalgia loose.
Places, things, and people she'd grown up with flooded her
mind, popping up like flotsam in a raging river. Green grass,
flowers, colored leaves in autumn. It's beautiful there, too.

Her mind went back to Fred. *I don't love him.*

But is love excitement of a touch—or the long, comfortable
companionship of years?

Tossing her head to clear the cobwebs, she read Priscilla's
letter again. The long descriptions of changes to the house
and assurance that nothing in her room would be changed
chased away the nostalgia and guilt took over.

She's afraid she'll hurt my feelings, Lori realized. *Tomorrow I'll write and tell her to make my old room into a nursery.
I'm not coming back.*

*Not coming back to Oak Ridge—or not coming back to
your old room?*

I don't know.

Lori turned out the light and sat listening to the wind in the trees, the water lapping the shore. The sounds took her back to their camp on Lake Ontario. The storms would come across the lake with thunder, lightning, rain, and wind. Her mother would hold her and tell stories, she remembered. *Mom and Dad had the kind of life Fred offers me. A safe place in the storm.* Had her mother known the thrill of love? Everyday her father drove to Oswego to work. Her mother went off to kindergarten to teach. *I don't ever remember not wanting to teach, just like Mom,* she thought. *A sudden patch of ice in a blinding snowstorm stole them away from me. Oh, Mom, I need you now. You could help me find the right answers.* Only the wind blowing across the bay answered her plaintive thoughts.

Fred had always been there. A safe five years older. . . wiser. An excuse when college friendships threatened to get too serious. The boyfriend back home routine chilled over-amorous advances.

You never used that line on Greg.

"Never had to," she moaned.

Good old Fred. He wasn't bad looking. In a tux at her sorority spring dance, he'd looked as handsome as Cindy's Dan. His kisses had stirred her, but. . .

"He's so stuffy." Lori flung herself out of the chair and went to the kitchen for something to eat.

Her refrigerator offered little more than light when she opened it. She sighed, remembering how carefully she'd planned meals for the O'Briens. "Oh, well," she comforted herself. "There's always peanut butter and jam."

With a cup of cocoa and a sandwich made with Greg's homemade bread, she went back to her office to work on lesson plans for the next week. She still had a stack of papers to grade from the hectic days of baby-sitting at the O'Briens'.

Fred's letter lay scattered on the living room floor. The paper might be forgotten, but the message burned in her memory. Lori tried to push private thoughts out of the way while she prepared school lessons. Finally giving up trying to concentrate, she took a long hot shower, braided her wet hair, and snuggled into bed.

The wind grew strong and nasty, bringing rain pounding against her trailer. Water gushed out of the downspout near her bedroom window. The sounds lulled her to sleep. Dreams of home kept her restless. The incongruous image of Greg dressed in a suit and acting as bank president sent her tossing until the still more ludicrous caricature of Fred in the logging camp woke her up.

Sensing something different, Lori sat up. A quiet question, "Meow?" issued from the foot of her bed.

"Marmalade?"

The fifteen-pound cat stretched, walked softly to the head of her bed, and pushed his head against her hand to be petted.

"You're right, Marmalade. I should become an old maid and raise cats instead of kids." She slid back under the covers, curled on her side with the cat fitted into the curve of her body, and fell into a sound sleep.

nine

Greg left for K.A.T.'s Kodiak office on Monday. His schedule would bring him back to Monk's on Thursday. Lori would take the same plane back to town. Her protests about leaving the school were silenced by Liz and Betty.

"You tell us what the kids are supposed to do and we'll see that it gets done. Liz will take care of the young ones and I'll keep the older students in line," Betty promised.

Lori checked her pack one more time. She'd be coming home by boat, so she carefully folded her clothes into a waterproof bag. *The Alaskan suitcase,* she said to herself. Marmalade sat on the foot of her bed, glaring at the open bag.

"Sorry, old man, you just won't fit." Lori stopped to scratch his head. "You have to stay home and take care of Greg." Silently she added, *While I go check out his girlfriend.*

Her mind filled with a jumble of thoughts. Fred's letter lay unanswered in her desk drawer. Lori couldn't bring herself to the point of saying no, cutting her last tie with the security of her old life.

You don't want to marry him.

What are the alternatives?

The stuffy sameness, day in and month out. You'd go mad.

Maybe. Might be better than not knowing what tomorrow will bring.

Just hope it isn't fog.

She folded the bag over, fastening the Velcro and tightening the straps with a vengeance that silenced her thoughts. The cat followed her when she went to the kitchen. She fixed his evening bowl of warm milk. The nights were too cold to leave the doors open. When Greg had to be away, she knew the tabby would stay with her. More and more often, even

115

when Greg stayed at home, she'd hear the familiar scratch on her back door at bedtime. Greg never mentioned his cat's wandering. Lori never told him where his pet stayed at night.

She and Marmalade settled down in her bed. Mentally, she went over the weekend plans again. She'd asked Greg to make motel reservations for her and she would rent a car at the airport. Thursday night she'd spend in Kodiak and fly to Uzinkie Friday afternoon. Weather reports were favorable and she prayed they would prove correct. She fell asleep listening to the cat purr and wondering about the schoolchildren she would meet.

At two o'clock the next afternoon, she heard the plane approach. Hastily she excused school, asking Scott, "Will you please stay and close up for me?"

Lori climbed into the plane she'd flown out on what seemed a lifetime ago. Now she wore the uniform of the country, jeans and a rag wool sweater. No more high heels, but for town she'd tossed aside rubber boots and wore brushed leather oxfords with thick crepe soles. She carried the once-hated down jacket tucked under her arm. Even the camera slung around her neck fit in. No one could live in paradise and not take pictures.

The flight proved quick and uneventful. Lori could see scattered islands between bits and pieces of light clouds and then Kodiak, climbing up the hill behind the marina, came into view. When she stepped off the plane, a freckle-faced redhead offered her his hand.

"Hi, Lori. Good to see you again."

She took a second look at the vaguely familiar face. "Oh, Joe."

A wide, friendly smile spread over his face. "You remember me."

"How did you know I'd be here?" she asked while she waited for Hal and his helper to unload the plane.

"Tom's in my Bible study group." Joe motioned toward the figure in coveralls helping Hal. "He mentioned Hal would be bringing the Monk's Island teacher to town. So here I am."

Lori didn't know what to say. This wasn't part of her plan, but months in Alaska had taught her to expect the unexpected.

"You in for the weekend?" Joe asked.

"No." She claimed her pack as Tom put it on the ground. "I'll be going to Uzinkie tomorrow."

"Hey, that doesn't give us much time." Before she could protest, he'd grabbed her bag and headed across the blacktopped runway, toward the parking lot. Flustered, Lori waved good-bye to Hal and followed the impetuous young man who had her belongings.

He led her to a battered orange Volkswagen and tossed her pack in the back. He then held the door for her.

"Where are we going?"

"You hungry? How about a pizza and pop?"

Lori could only blink. . .pizza and pop. . .the real world! Her mouth started to water. "Sounds great," she said tentatively. Joe's car roared to life, and Lori watched as the road wound away from the Coast Guard base and the airport, leading them toward houses and stores. It seemed a long way to town for someone used to running a few hundred feet from one end of "town" to the other. Her companion kept a steady flow of chatter going, pointing out places of interest as they drove.

"Where are you staying?" he inquired.

"Got a reservation at the Kodiak Inn."

"Want to drop your stuff off first?"

"Okay."

"You could stay at my place. I've got two bedrooms."

"Thanks, I'll be fine here. Can I rent a car nearby?" She looked at the businesses around her.

"No need. You can use mine. Theresa says it runs great."

"Thanks. I'd be glad to give you the rental money," she offered.

"Don't be silly. You buy your own gas and we'll call it even."

Joe carried her pack into the motel office for her. She

checked in and wrote a check for payment. She never used real money anymore. Her paycheck went to the bank and she wrote checks to pay what bills she had.

"Want me to wait here?" Joe asked as the clerk handed Lori her room key.

Lori sighed in relief. She didn't feel comfortable having a man follow her to a motel room. "I'll be right back," she promised, grabbing her bag.

Two hours later she sat back, relaxed and full. "Ahhh, junk food! How I've missed it."

She found Joe fun. His light banter and stories about friends and adventures in the Coast Guard kept her entertained. "You want to drive around? See the sights of Kodiak?" he offered.

She blinked, looked out the window, and exclaimed, "It's dark."

"Ever hear of electricity? I even have television at my place."

Lori giggled. "Never heard of it."

The evening passed in a blur of excitement reminiscent of college days. She met several of Joe's friends. Some of them wound up at his trailer looking at TV.

"Want more coffee?"

"If I'm going to find my way back to town tonight, I better start now."

Joe pulled the car keys out of his pocket. "Come on, I'll show you some of the Orange Bug's idiosyncrasies."

She said good-bye to the people she'd met and followed Joe out to the car. Before she got in the car, he gave her a friendly hug.

"I haven't had so much fun in ages," she told him.

"Don't wait so long to come back."

She covered the miles to her motel feeling mellow. *Must be the junk food,* she reasoned.

Could be you've let go of your problems.

Joe's fun. He's not afraid of women. Wonder if he can bake bread? She giggled as she parked his Volks by her motel.

&

Friday found her up early and wandering through stores. *I've never really looked at a grocery store before,* she thought, as she pushed a cart up and down the aisle.

"Can I get this delivered to Monk's Island?"

"Sure. Just getting the orders ready to run to the airport. Be a plane out today."

And I'll be on it, Lori mused, idly watching the box boy deftly packing her groceries. As he worked, she wandered over to look at a display of gift items. She spotted blocks of chocolate with figures imprinted of eagles, otter, deer, and other creatures of the country. *Peggy, Mark, and Aaron,* she thought and picked up three. She paid for them and dropped them into her bag.

Time flew and she regretted not planning to spend another day in town as she repacked her bag and headed for the airport. "When you'd like to get weathered in, the sky stays clear," she muttered, looking at the fluffy white clouds floating above.

She parked Joe's car in the agreed spot, hid the key under the seat with a note of thanks, and headed toward the familiar blue and white amphibious plane. She climbed up to the co-pilot spot by Hal. He would stop by Uzinkie on his way to Monk's Island.

"How you getting home?" he asked her as they waited to be cleared for takeoff.

"Greg's coming over by boat on Sunday."

Hal scowled. "Bad time of year to depend on a small boat." He checked his instruments one more time. "But Greg's boat is bigger than a Bidarka."

The clear weather made flying a pleasure. As Hal circled in over Spruce Island, he pointed ahead to a large tree-covered island on the horizon. "That's Afognak Island," he yelled over the engine noise.

Lori strained to see as they taxied over the water toward the village. There were houses of all kinds and colors marching up the slope away from the water. Her nerves tingled as Hal pulled up to the large floating dock. She looked around apprehensively at the circle of waiting faces as she climbed out of the plane.

"Lori?"

Turning, she recognized the small, dark woman who spoke as the one in the picture Greg had. "Yes," Lori nodded.

"I'm Rika, Greg's little sister."

Little sister? Her mind tried to absorb this bit of news while she greeted the young native. The girl's short dark brown hair feathered around her attractive face. Almost black eyes showed warmth and welcome. Lori reached out to shake hands. Looking at the assembled people, she realized most were her same height. *I'll fit right in here,* she thought, as she smiled to the gathered group.

"Come, I'll take you to Kalissa."

Lori motioned toward her pack, but before she could speak, Rika told her, "Nikita will bring it."

"Are you the teacher here?" Lori asked her hostess.

Rika smiled. "Yes, tomorrow you'll meet my pupils. They've planned a party for you."

Lori walked over the stone beach, looking and trying to assimilate all she saw. A couple houses looked like they could use some care. Others were lovely, with decks looking over the water. She could see planters that must be full of colorful flowers in summer. Rika led her to a small blue frame house she'd seen from the dock.

"We live here."

"You live with Kalissa?"

Rika nodded. "She had a mild stroke a couple years ago. That coupled with her age made us decide she shouldn't be alone."

Lori followed Rika into what appeared to be a kitchen and sitting room. Kalissa reached out to Lori as soon as she came through the door. Lori noted the dark parchment stretched over the round head of the old woman. Her features showed her Mongolian ancestors. Sitting down, Kalissa didn't appear so tiny, but when she rose to greet Lori, she stood less than five feet tall. Lori took the gnarled hand in her own.

"You Greeg's teacher?" She spoke the name like a musical note.

"I teach in the logging camp on Monk's Island."

"We talk now." She led Lori to a chair near her own. "You drink chi?"

Lori looked to Rika, who nodded yes. Kalissa settled her old bones in the one overstuffed chair by the wood heater and Lori sat on a wooden chair nearby. "My Greeg good boy."

Rika put a small table next to Lori and brought cups of tea for each of them.

"This is chi," she said softly as she set Lori's cup down. Then she pulled another wooden chair near Lori's and sat down. "Tell us how you got here, Kalissa." She spoke in a clear and loud voice. Lori realized Kalissa must be a bit deaf.

The nearly black eyes looked from one girl to the other. "You want to know about Greeg?"

Rika put her hand lovingly over Kalissa's. "We want to know about you."

"My village long way off." Her small hand fluttered, motioning into space.

"She grew up in the Aleutians," Rika whispered.

"We fish, hunt, follow spirits." She looked at the girls, but Lori felt sure her mind was back in her childhood.

"Kot-le-wah, good man, good hunter."

"Her husband," Rika explained.

Kalissa's small body heaved a great sigh. "But big boats come. Kot-le-wah hunting. Not there and mens take me away." Her eyes filled with tears. "I not see him again."

"How cruel." It hurt Lori to see this old woman grieve.

"The story is always the same. Greg and I heard it many times growing up and finally found out what happened." Rika stopped to look at Kalissa, who sat staring into space, her cup forgotten in her hand.

"It happened during World War Two. No one had ever paid much attention to the Aleutians until they realized many people in Alaska live closer to the capital of Japan than they do to Alaska's capital in Juneau. Some feared an invasion, so many people were evacuated. Kalissa was sent to a camp in southeast Alaska. We could never prove it, but we're sure Kot-le-wah was taken prisoner. The Japanese did take Aleuts prisoners from Attu. They kept them on their island of Hokkaido. Even when the prisoners were released, Kot-le-wah never came back."

"I not see Kot-le-wah again," the old lady whispered sadly.

"You have many children now."

Lori watched the wrinkled face beam with happiness. "I come back Kodiak. Sometimes work cannery, most time work for white ladies."

Rika turned to Lori. "We don't know how long she stayed on the panhandle, but we've found people in Kodiak who she worked for in the fifties."

"Ilsa my friend. She make home for me and I cook for her . . .take care of Greeg." Kalissa's eyes glowed with love.

Lori looked at Rika, who nodded. "She did housework and laundry. She lived with Greg's parents as housekeeper for them."

"How did she get to keep Greg?"

The young woman giggled. "She kidnapped him."

"What?" This sounded bazaar to Lori.

"Greg's had the records straightened out now, but somehow when his parents' boat went down, he was listed as having gone down with it. Lucky for him, his mother had written Olga in Seattle saying she'd left Greg with their housekeeper while she acted as cook on the family's boat. Olga didn't have the money to come to Alaska, so she wrote to the authorities and sent copies of the letters. It raised enough of a question that the Jensens' estate was put in trust. Olga tried to find Greg and Kalissa, but she could do very little by mail."

"I bring Greeg here. He grow up hunter like Kot-le-wah."

"He must have looked like Gulliver in Lilliput," Lori exclaimed, thinking of the blond giant among the short dark people.

Rika laughed. "We've got enough Russian ancestors so not all of us look alike." She got up to pour more tea. "Are you warm enough?" she asked Kalissa, refilling her cup.

"Oh." Lori jumped up. "I've got a present for you." Her pack sat just inside the door, where a young man had set it down, waved to Kalissa, and disappeared. Hastily, Lori opened it and took out the bright red and white lap robe Betty had crocheted for her. She brought it back and tucked it around Kalissa's waist, draping it over the thin legs.

"Nice. You make this?"

Lori shook her head. "My friend made it."

Kalissa held up her hands. "I make sweaters. Now my hands no work."

Taking the tiny frail hands in her own, Lori leaned down to brush her lips over them.

"You nice. You for my Greeg?"

Her face felt hot and tears burned her eyes. Lori couldn't speak; she saw Rika, and through a blur thought, *She's what he wants.*

Kalissa smiled and folded her hands back in her lap. "He go back to his people."

Rika spoke loudly from where she worked at the sink. "No, he didn't. You wanted him to go to school and he did, but he belongs here. He came back."

Every word pierced Lori's heart.

After putting a pan on the stove, the native girl came back to sit down and continue her story. "Kalissa brought Greg here as soon as she knew his parents were dead. We don't know why the authorities couldn't find him. Maybe they didn't look. He was twelve before Olga found him. Did he tell you about her?"

"Only that she was his mother's friend."

"She's his mother's sister. She could have claimed his parents' money when the authorities couldn't find Greg. She never gave up looking for him and kept the money for him."

Lori remembered his anger when he spoke of the money. She didn't remember his saying much about Olga and certainly not that she was his aunt.

"It took her five years of searching. She saved her money and came to Kodiak to talk to old neighbors of the Jensens'. Through friends of her sister, she found Greg here with Kalissa. She wanted to take him home with her. They got as far as Kodiak and Greg ran away. She knew he would come back to Kalissa. She gave up and went back to Seattle. She arranged for the trust to send money to Kalissa each month and she wrote to Greg."

"I not need money."

"Not even with all your children?"

Kalissa smiled a toothless smile.

Rika looked to Lori. "My people love children. If a parent dies, there are dozens who will take the children. Kalissa has collected many of us." Her look of love warmed Lori. "How many, Kalissa?" Rika asked.

"You come. You go. I no count."

Rika rose, hugged Kalissa, and went to check the stove. Good smells wafted toward Lori, reminding her she hadn't eaten lunch.

"May I help?"

"You can set the table."

Kalissa dozed in her chair while the girls got ready for supper.

"How old is she?" Lori asked.

Rika shrugged. "We think mid to late seventies. There weren't birth certificates where she was born." She pulled a bubbling casserole from the oven. "She's raised a dozen of us and we all remember her as old." Looking wistfully at her foster mother she added, "Greg's her favorite. She's failed ever since he left home."

"That's ten years," Lori said in wonder.

Nodding, Rika continued to stir vegetables. "I was fourteen when he left and there were still two younger ones. She didn't take any more after that."

Lori looked at the closed eyes and the shriveled body and whispered, "She's a wonder."

"That she is."

Supper tasted good and Lori ate hungrily. She felt drawn to the quiet-spoken, friendly young woman. She could understand why Greg would love her. Rika and Kalissa teased each other, while Lori enjoyed sitting back and listening to them talk about the different children who had grown up under this roof.

"The boys slept upstairs. It's like what you call an attic or loft. We girls lined up cots in there." Rika pointed to one of the rooms opening off the kitchen–sitting room. "You sleep in Greg's bed?"

Lori started in shock. "No, no," she protested.

Rika dissolved in laughter. Struggling to control herself, she hiccuped, "Sorry. I start talking in Kalissa's shorthand." She brushed her short cropped hair from her face. "I meant, would you like to be by yourself and sleep in Greg's bed in the loft?"

"Not if he's in it."

That sent Rika into more gales of laughter. Kalissa smiled happily. Lori wasn't sure if the old lady understood what was going on or not.

"Let's clear up this mess. We'll decide on sleeping arrangements later." Rika rose, helped Kalissa back to her chair, and put more wood in the stove.

Lori started stacking the dishes. While they finished up the household duties, the girls talked about teaching.

"Sounds like we have the same problems." Lori hung up the dish towel.

"Kids come in different colors, but underneath they're the same," Rika said.

"Why do you teach here?" Lori inquired.

"I owe Greg." Rika put the dishpan away and went to Kalissa. "You ready for bed?"

The little woman got out of her chair. She patted Lori's face. "We talk tomorrow."

Thoughts of all she'd heard filled Lori's mind as she sat in the quiet room. The sounds were the same as home. The wind and the waves lulled her. Faint sounds of Rika putting Kalissa to bed broke into her reverie.

"She sleeps a lot. Catching up for all the years we thought she never slept," Rika said, sitting on a wooden chair. She wiggled a bit. "This isn't comfortable. Come on."

Lori followed her into the other bedroom. The two beds were covered with matching pink print spreads. Sheer ruffled white curtains framed the windows and paintings of flowers decorated the walls. "This is beautiful."

"Thanks. Kalissa won't change the rest of the house. Greg had to tie her down to get the new wood heater installed. We never believed she'd use the chair he bought her. Me," she waved around her room, "I like nice things."

"Who did the paintings?" Lori asked, going closer to the pictures.

"I did," came the soft answer.

"They're very good. What kind of flowers are these?" Lori looked at the bright blossoms.

"Anemones. They bloom in the early summer."

Lori plopped down on one of the beds. "I've got so much to learn about this place. I haven't even started on the plant life."

"When will you go home?"

Surprised, Lori answered, "Sunday. Greg's coming after me."

Rika giggled. "I mean back south."

Both girls kicked their shoes off. Lori sat cross-legged on one bed and Rika on the other. "I'm not sure I want to go back south. You came back home to teach. Do you like it?"

"For a while." Rika ran her finger over the pattern in the bedspread. "At least as long as Kalissa needs me."

"May I ask a personal question?"

"Sure." Rika looked up.

"Earlier you said you stayed because you owed Greg."

"That's right. Greg thinks everyone should stay where they grew up. . .go back to the village." She continued tracing the flowers in the bedspread. "I think he's caught between two worlds. . .not sure where he belongs, so he tells us we should cling to our heritage." She looked up again. "He'd howl if he heard me say it, but he tries to pay us to do what he wants."

"Pay you!"

"Greg's got all that money from his parents."

"He told me about it."

"Did he tell you he wants to put every kid in the village through college?"

"Really?"

"The catch is you have to come back here to work. He found out he had to go outside to find the work he studied for—so to be fair, he only asks us to stay a year."

"When your year's up, will you marry him?" Lori's throat felt tight and her words pinched, but she had to know.

Rika fell backwards on the bed and rocked in glee. "Marry Greg?" She sat up, hiccuping in suppressed laughter. "He's a grouch."

Lori shook her head. "Aren't you his girlfriend?"

Rika went into another spasm of giggles. "He's bossed me most of my life. Next spring I'll marry Nikita, and Greg will give me away." She hiccuped, "I hope he realizes that means he has to quit telling me how to live my life."

"But," Lori scowled, trying to understand what she'd heard, "he has a girlfriend here."

"He calls Kalissa his girl." She still hiccuped from her fit of giggles. Her face became serious. "You love him, don't you?"

Lori swallowed over the lump in her throat. "I think so." Her voice came out so softly she could barely hear it herself.

Rika jumped off her bed and sat next to Lori. "Does he know?" She put an arm around Lori.

Lori shook her head. "He told me he has no time for women."

Slapping her hand against the bed, Rika growled deep in her throat. "I could shake him until his hair falls out. He is so stubborn. Why can't he act normal? Says he's native. Why can't he see how white he is, inside and out."

Lori watched in wonder, drawn to this kindred spirit.

"My people live close to nature. They are warm, alive, human." Her dark eyes flashed. "He acts like a dead fish."

Feeling something close to hope rise, Lori said, "I thought it must be me. He treats me like I was his sister."

"That bad!"

It was Lori's turn to giggle in spite of herself. "He kisses me on the forehead like I was a little girl."

"Always?"

The blush would not be held back. Nodding her head, she put her hands over her hot cheeks. "He told me he has no time for women," she whispered, letting her hands drop.

Rika gave her a quick hug, then started to loosen Lori's hair. "May I?"

"Cindy used to brush my hair." Lori turned her back to Rika. "She was my roommate in college."

As Rika started to brush, she asked, "Does Greg talk about A-ly-as-ka?"

Puzzled, Lori answered slowly, "No."

"More Aleut words for you to learn. It means, the great land."

"He talks a lot about native Alaskans and wanting to work for them."

"All we need. Another do-gooder."

Lori's head tipped back with the angry pull on the brush.

"Wish he'd find himself. Make his own life and stop preaching."

"Greg preach? He's not even a believer." As the brushing continued, so did she. "Do all his brothers and sisters feel this way?"

Rika stopped brushing. "You must think me ungrateful. Truth is, I love Greg. He's my big brother and I'd like to see him happy."

"I feel that way about my brother, too. I didn't realize until I came here that he is happy. My jealousy of his wife blinded me to his happiness," Lori admitted.

The brushing started again. "Maybe Greg's jealous of

Nikita and me. We've been sweethearts for years. I know Greg thought I would quit college and come home." She giggled. "We fooled him. Nikita won a scholarship and came to college with me. Someday we'll teach in the same school. The Alaskan Native Service schools like to hire couples. Kind of like getting two for the price of one."

"Where will you live when you're married?"

"Here. I won't leave Kalissa. There are others she's cared for who would come, but I want to stay with her and Nikita understands."

"When will I get to meet him?"

"Tomorrow. We have a party, remember?" The brushing stopped. "Wow, look at the time. If we don't get to bed, it will be time to get up before we fall asleep."

"Like college, when we talked all night."

"You did that, too?"

It seemed to Lori she had been friends with this girl forever. The attraction was more than knowing someone who'd grown up with Greg. Rika seemed more like a sister than even Cindy had been.

≈

Saturday dawned bright and clear. All morning Kalissa told Lori stories of raising her children. She had many memories of Greg to share. Rika slipped out to help her students prepare a celebration to greet Lori, leaving the two to get better acquainted. When Rika returned at noon, Kalissa was tired.

"I take a nap. You two go off. . .have fun."

The girls fixed her a lunch. Then they helped her back to her chair and tucked her new robe around her legs. "Will she be all right alone?" Lori asked.

"She's alone all day while I teach. She'll just doze in her chair until we get back."

Kalissa didn't attend the party, but Lori felt sure everyone else in the village did. She had never felt such a warm welcome. The children crowded around her, talking, laughing, and vying for her attention. Each of them had a gift for her.

She oohed and aahed over everything from crayoned

drawings to a beautifully knit cap made by one of the senior girls. "I will treasure them all and I will wear the hat every day." She promptly pulled the colorful cap over her long hair.

"No, no, Miss Wilson. Don't cover your hair." Lori had done her hair in a knot in an attempt to look more dressy for the party. When she pulled the cap off, her hair came tumbling down her back. The older girls giggled and begged to help braid her hair as they had seen it done when she'd arrived on the plane. It was like being surrounded by lots of younger sisters.

Nikita had claimed Rika as soon as the girls arrived at the schoolhouse where the gathering was held. He had the same straight brown hair as Rika, but his eyes were more brown than her nearly black ones. He stood taller than most of the men in the village, but Lori knew Greg would tower over everyone. Rika's face glowed when she walked hand in hand with Nikita. He looked back at her with obvious love. Watching them, Lori knew she would never be content to marry Fred. The security Fred offered came with a price tag higher than she wanted to pay.

Lori didn't have much time to watch the lovers. The children claimed all her attention. They proudly showed her their school papers and grinned happily when she praised their work. She sang songs with them, listened to their stories, and the day seemed to vanish. The men had prepared a huge salmon barbecue. The women piled the tables with more food than twice as many hungry people could eat. Darkness had claimed the day when Rika and Lori piled a plate with leftover food to take to Kalissa.

"You laugh. Sound like my children come home," Kalissa greeted them. She patted Lori's hand. "You be mine, too?"

"I'd like that, Kalissa."

"You have mother?"

Lori pulled her chair close where she could hold the tiny wrinkled hand. "No, my parents died."

"You stay here?"

"Greg will take me back to Monk's Island tomorrow."

The gray head bobbed. "You stay A-ly-as-ka?"

"Your great land." Lori looked out the window toward the water and spoke her thoughts aloud. "Yes, Kalissa, I'll stay in your great land."

ten

Greg arrived about noon and insisted they leave by two. If he noticed the warmth between Rika and Lori, he said nothing.

"Weather's turning and I want to get across Marmont Bay before the wind gets worse," he explained when he insisted on leaving so soon.

Rika shook her head and whispered in Lori's ear, "Told you he's a grouch."

Greg walked into the house and Kalissa's frail body seemed to crackle with newfound energy. Her face radiated love for her adopted son. Greg showed a gentle, loving manner Lori had not thought him capable of.

"I cook you chi."

Kalissa's tiny body disappeared in his hug. "I make the chi, you sit like a lady." Greg picked her up like a doll, carried her to her chair, and tucked the lap robe around her.

"Nice girl bring me." The wrinkled hand patted the red and white yarn. Her eyes twinkled with mischief. "Why you no bring Lor-ee before?"

"You no like white girls," he teased, giving her ear a smooch.

Kalissa grabbed Lori's hand when she set down the cup of tea Rika had made. "She my girl."

Greg's eyes held a deep, warm glow when he looked at Lori. Her heart stopped and she held her breath. *He is capable of love,* her mind shouted.

But he's not a Christian, her conscience answered.

Nikita came by and the men talked about boats, motors, and fishing. The girls fixed lunch. Lori didn't want the visit to end.

"My bones say bad storm. You go soon?" Kalissa asked as the girls cleared the table.

Greg held the frail little woman one more time. "Your old

bones feel rheumatism, not a storm. We'll be home in a little over an hour. Wind was against me coming over, so it took longer. It'll be blowing right to push us back."

Rika and Lori had packed all Lori's gifts in a box and carefully wrapped it in plastic bags to keep her treasures dry.

"I brought your boots and rain gear. They're in the boat," Greg told her when she brought her pack out of the girls' bedroom.

With many promises of a quick return, Lori bid Kalissa good-bye. Rika and Nikita walked Lori and Greg to the boat. The men took the small motor off and carried it to Nikita's workshop. "I'll have it in tiptop shape before you come back," Nikita promised.

Lori shivered in the cold as the girls waited for the men to return. Clouds hung low and threatening.

"You better dig out that rain gear and get it on," Rika advised. "It will break the windchill even if the rain doesn't hit until after you get home."

Greg and Nikita returned and Nikita started to put Lori's pack under the front seat. "What all this junk?" he asked Greg.

"Got a new tarp last time I was in Kodiak. Getting winter and I'll need it to keep the boat and motors covered."

"Bring the boat back over and I'll winterize the big motor, too," Nikita offered.

While the men talked mechanics and motors, the women made promises to write and visit.

"You'll come soon to see Monk's Island?"

Rika motioned with her head at Greg. "Get big brother to fly me over." She hugged herself and shivered. "I think traveling by boat went out with Bidarkas."

With a final hug and kiss, Lori climbed in the boat and called good-bye as Nikita untied them from the dock.

Greg had refueled in Uzinkie and the smell of gasoline assaulted Lori's nose. The motor coughed once and then started. Lori and Greg waved to the couple on the dock and Greg set a course for home.

"Going straight across. It will be rough, so we'll take it slow and easy," he yelled to Lori over the sound of the motor.

Lori relaxed on her seat behind him. She had dressed warm, even putting on the long johns Rika had insisted on. She pulled her new wool cap over her braided hair. The down jacket felt warm under the neoprene rain clothes. She watched Greg, standing at the controls in his mustang suit. The heavy orange coveralls were the latest thing in survival gear. She wondered if they were as warm as he claimed they were.

She wiggled her toes inside her boots. She hadn't remembered wool socks so she'd worn two pairs of regular socks. *Should only be an hour or two,* she told herself, settling back for the rough ride.

The wind seemed to pull at her clothes. The waves looked dark, angry, and forbidding. *Greg's made this trip hundreds of times. No reason to worry,* she told herself, saying a prayer for their safe trip. The rain started coming down in a steady downpour. Lori watched the streams run off her rain pants and mentally thanked Greg for remembering to bring her rain gear.

When she looked up, it seemed the clouds were so low she could reach out and touch them. The boat crashed into a wave and Lori took a faceful of salt spray. Greg slowed the motor as the water became more choppy. He looked back at Lori and she could read his concern.

"I'm fine," she shouted. She and Bob had taken some reckless chances on Lake Ontario. The thrill of challenging the elements ran high. She watched as Greg held the bow into the waves. Each crash into the trough sent a shiver of excitement tingling through her. A small nudge of fear skirted her mind, but the roar of the motor behind her quelled it.

The comforting roar sputtered. Lori immediately turned to watch the prop. *We must be bouncing it right out of the water,* she thought. She looked back to Greg, smiling in spite of the rain hitting her face. His look wiped the smile away. Fear gripped her.

She pushed it back; he's just being a grouch again.

But the motor didn't sound right.

She looked at the prop. . .it wasn't there. The bow dipped, and when the stern rose out of the water, she could see the prop was gone.

The boat swung at the same time she looked at Greg. She pointed frantically. "It's gone," she screamed.

"I can't hold it."

"The prop's gone." The boat rocked precariously in the rough water.

Greg nearly fell and grabbed her shoulder to steady himself. "Are you sure?"

Anger mixed with fear. "I know what a prop looks like and we don't have one," she yelled as he bent over her to look into the water.

The motor idled uselessly. Greg stumbled back and turned it off. He grabbed the paddle and vainly tried to hold the boat into the waves.

"Where are we?"

Greg glanced at the compass mounted on the console, "Not sure."

"Oh my God," Lori prayed, fighting back the terror in her throat.

The fog lay like a blanket over the water. Without the motor to propel them, the boat bucked and weaved at the mercy of the wind and waves. Rain fell steadily as Greg struggled with the paddle.

"Can I help?" she asked.

"No. Are you all right?"

"Depends on how far I have to swim."

He swung around to look at her. She smiled and watched his face relax in answer to her grin. "You scared?" His voice held concern.

"If it will help, I'll be terrified."

"The wind seems to be shifting. We're out in open water and I'm not sure yet where we're drifting."

The boat slid into a trough. Lori shivered. "Will we go over?" she asked, gripping the side of the boat.

"Nope. This boat is designed not to tip over."

"Promises, promises," she muttered as they rocked over the crest into a still deeper trough. Moments passed like hours. Too numb to think, Lori kept repeating the Lord's Prayer over and over under her breath. Greg tried to steer with the paddle, holding it deep in the water to swing the boat around. Lori stared into the murk searching for land.

"Look!" She pointed to a dark shadow.

He turned to follow where her finger pointed. A brief break in the fog showed the outline of trees. "How far?" she whispered.

"I'm not sure if we're even drifting that way."

"Oh, please, Lord," Lori prayed. She strained to see the land as the fog blinked it in and out of her vision.

Greg pulled hard on the paddle, swinging the boat around toward the surf they could hear. Ever so slowly they got closer and closer to the sound of waves crashing on land. Rocks loomed ahead. "There, see that break in the rocks? We'll try to land there."

"What do you want me to do?"

Greg swung the paddle to the other side of the boat. "Landing in this surf will be rough. If you can hold the boat straight, I'll jump out and pull us ashore."

Lori saw the spot he pointed to. The surf pounded against rocks all the way to the beach. *It looks so small,* she thought, eyeing the break in the rocks that loomed out of the water whenever the waves receded. Standing, she took the paddle from Greg.

She moved to the console as he climbed to the bow of the boat, ready to jump. The huge waves pushed them closer and closer. Greg watched the action of the water.

"Now!" he shouted, jumping over the bow of the boat.

Lori dug the paddle in on the same side he jumped on as the breaker hit them with tremendous force.

Crack! Lori fell backward, still clutching the broken paddle handle. She scrambled to her feet in time to see Greg pinned against the rocks by the boat. Without thought, she leaped over the bow of the boat, grabbed the bowline, and watched for the next wave.

As it hit, she pulled with all her strength to use the force of the water to bring the boat straight onto the shore. She grabbed the side of the boat and prepared to pull again. She expected Greg to take the opposite side and help her. Looking for him she saw him slowly getting to his feet. "Are you hurt?"

"Twisted my ankle. Here, let me help." He tried to take hold of the boat. Lori watched in horror as his face went white and he groaned in pain. A wave hit the back of the boat, throwing spray over both of them.

"Try to get up on the beach. I'll take care of the boat," she yelled. As the next wave crashed into the back of the boat, she heaved again, bringing the bow onto the beach.

Greg stood close enough to the boat to grab hold, and with the next wave they managed to get the boat more than half out of the water.

"What's the tide?"

"High," he answered. "Can you tie the bowline to something? That will keep it from drifting back out."

"Sure. Can you walk at all?"

He tested his foot and hopped a couple steps on his good leg. She tied the rope to a rock and came back to him. "Here, hold on to me."

Greg took hold of her shoulder and hopped to where he could sit on a fallen log. "I got caught in the rocks. Couldn't get my foot loose and the boat knocked me down."

"My fault. The paddle broke and I couldn't keep the boat from swinging in on you."

"Hey, you did okay. Quick thinking on your part to get the boat beached."

"Do you think it's broken?" She looked at his boot-clad foot but could tell nothing.

"I don't know. Maybe you better get the anchor out and set it up behind those rocks, too."

"All right. Then we'll see what we can do about your ankle." Running back to the boat, she pushed aside the tarp and other gear blocking the bucket that held the anchor and rope. She managed to haul the anchor to the rocks and wedge the prongs behind a large boulder. She made sure the anchor rope held secure to the boat before going back to Greg.

She saw him shiver. "Are you cold?" *Shelter,* she thought, *got to get shelter before he goes into shock.*

He pulled his mustang suit hood over his head. "My suit will keep me warm. What about you?"

She grinned. "I'm sweating with all these clothes and running in the rocks." She pointed to the boat. "Do you think the tide will come up this far?"

"No. Tide's high now and you've done a good job getting the boat above the waterline. Now can you manage to get the tarp?"

She looked beyond the rocks to the tree line. "Let me check out what's available first. Will you be okay?"

"Hey, I'm fine. Just can't walk too well. What do you plan to do?"

"I want to see if I can find a spot where we can rig that tarp into a tent. Can you dig out that trusty knife of yours?"

"You planning on cutting down a tree?" He tried to smile, but she could see the pain etched in his face.

"No, just rope. Sit tight. I'll be right back." She walked over the rocks to where the beach rose to trees and brush. "Might work," she said to the wind.

She hurried back to Greg. "I found a couple trees that I think we can get rope strung between. Do you think you could get that far?" She pointed to the edge of the forest. "You're tall and could get the rope up high."

"You go get the tarp and rope and I'll see what I can do."

She pulled the rolled, blue plastic out of the boat. "This is heavy," she puffed. She tried to pull a coil of rope loose and decided to come back for it. She lugged her heavy burden up the beach. Greg stood on one foot watching her.

"I'll take this up to the trees and go get the rope. Then I'll help you up to the trees."

"Yes, ma'am."

She felt the blush and remembered how upset she'd been

with him when he gave abrupt orders. Hurrying back with the rope over her shoulder, she offered him the other shoulder as a crutch. Slowly they made their way toward the trees. His clenched teeth and heavy breathing told her what an effort it was for him to move his injured leg.

"There, see those trees? If we can get a rope between them, I can use it as a base for the tarp."

He paused to lean against the first tree. "Okay, hand me the rope." He reached to put the rope over a branch and tie it tight. "Now let's see if I can make it to that one." He pointed to the second tree about eight feet away.

He used his knife to cut the rope and pulled it taut before tying it off on the second tree. "Now what?"

"I'm going to throw the tarp over and use the excess on the ends to tie to those trees in the back. Do you think I can get the long side of the tarp up there and then fold it under so we don't have to sit on wet ground?"

"Maybe you can anchor the long side with rocks before you fold it under. We seem to have lots of those."

She struggled with the huge heavy plastic. Greg tried to help where he could. He pulled the tarp over the line for her. Then he cut short lengths of rope for her to thread through the metal eyes in the edge of the tarp. She used the other end of these ropes to tie to trees to make a small shelter.

By the time she'd carried rocks to put on the inside of the tarp to spread it away from the line between the trees, she felt exhausted. Pulling the excess plastic inside made a floor over the carpet of moss and needles under the trees. She sank down on it. "Can you manage to get inside?"

Greg hopped to the edge of the "floor," where he sat down and scooted inside their makeshift shelter. "Where'd you learn to do this?"

"As kids we used to use blankets to make tents in the backyard. Only there we used Mom's clothesline and clothespins. Not as heavy as all this plastic."

He pointed to where the wind rattled the tightly tied tarp. "This will keep out the wind and the rain." He winced in pain as he tried to find a comfortable spot for his big frame.

"Will someone be looking for us?"

"They expect us back at Monk's tonight. When we don't show up, Jim will call the Coast Guard."

She looked out the small opening she'd left in the end of their shelter. The dark clouds hid what little daylight remained. "We may be here awhile." She spoke softly.

"Are you afraid?" He touched her cheek.

"No. I know the Lord will take care of us."

"You really believe, don't you?"

She nodded. "Without faith there is no life." She started out the opening. "Before the light is completely gone, I want to see what else we can use from the boat."

"There's a flashlight under the console."

"That will help, and I'll get the thermos of coffee Rika sent with us."

"Trust my little sister to think of coffee."

"She is special." Lori crawled out into the rain and wind.

She found the flashlight first and used it to forage in the bow of the boat. She brought her pack and the thermos back to the shelter, using the flashlight as a guide. "Want some coffee?"

"I'm really thirsty."

"Maybe the hot liquid will make you feel better. Then I'll put the thermos outside to catch rainwater for tomorrow."

"We should have a fire."

"Everything is so wet and it's too dark to do much tonight."

"You're right. We have to spare the batteries in the flashlight."

"Here, drink some coffee and I'll turn the light off. When I get used to the dark, I'll see what I can do about a fire." She held the cup out to him.

"We'll share. You've done the work and need something warm, too."

"You drink first. I want to get some stuff out of my pack. Maybe I can make a pillow for you. Would it help to have your leg up on something?"

"I think we're going to have to get the boot off before it swells any more."

"Oh." She shuddered inside, knowing she never did well at nursing. *Please, Lord, I need help to get through this.* She took the cup and refilled it, sipping on the warm coffee and thinking to herself.

"You're being quiet. Are you all right?"

"I'm praying, if you must know. Started to run a little low on courage and needed to ask God for a booster shot."

"Do you suppose He could manage a shot for pain while He's at it?"

"You really hurt a lot, don't you?"

"Before I lose all of my courage and while you've got a new supply, could we get this boot off?"

She felt around his leg and ankle. "Do you have that knife handy? I think it will be better if I cut this off."

He tried to sit up. "My leg?"

"No, silly, the boot."

She thanked God it was too dark for Greg to see her face as she sawed at the rubber boot. She knew it hurt him even though she tried to be gentle. Finally the boot came loose.

His groan told her all she needed to know. "The leg must be broken. At least the bone is not through the flesh."

"Thank you, Doctor Wilson," he gasped.

She pulled a sweater out of her pack and rolled it to fit under his leg. Greg barely fit in the makeshift tent. His head pressed against the end she'd tied around the trees to close off one side, and his feet were just inside the other end. His breathing became less ragged. "Does that feel better?"

"Yes. The swelling made the pressure against the boot painful. Can you find a comfortable spot? Do I take up too much room?"

"I admit when we made tents as kids I didn't have to share it with a giant." She tried to move. "I feel like the abominable snowman in all these clothes."

"Without a fire it's going to be cold tonight. Do we have something you can use as a blanket?"

"I'm going out now to see what I can forage up for a fire. Do we have matches?"

"There's a survival pack under the console. There should be dry matches in there."

"Any chance there would be some medicine you could use?"

"Not sure what's in it."

She picked up the flashlight. "I'll see what I can find."

"You could use some of the motor oil to get a fire started. Be better if you could manage to siphon off some gasoline."

"I'll try to gather wood first. I flunked fire making in Girl Scouts, so we may be in trouble."

When Lori crawled out of the shelter, she was hit by wind and rain. She made her way back to the boat and found the survival pack. She stuffed it inside her jacket without opening it. Next, she started picking up any small pieces of wood she could find close to their tent. "Here's the survival stuff." She tossed it to Greg. "Maybe you can see well enough to find anything we can use."

She went farther and farther along the beach, picking up wood and hauling it back toward the tent. Her night vision improved as she worked her way back and forth, adding more and more to her stack. The sheets of rain whipping across her face caused more discomfort than falling over unseen rocks. Finally, she made her way back to the boat to find a can of oil.

It seemed like hours before she dragged her tired body back inside the shelter. "Do we have matches?"

"Yes, and we have a spare blanket you can wrap up in. Once you quit all this work, you're going to feel the cold."

"Thanks, I can hardly wait. Now let me see what I can do about the fire."

Greg raised up on one arm to watch her. "Maybe I can hold the flashlight for you."

"Okay. I got a lot of wood, but it's all so wet."

"Start small. A few pieces piled up like a tepee will get it going. Did you get some gasoline?"

"No, but I did bring a can of oil." She pulled it out of the pocket of her raincoat. "Could you open it, please?"

She piled the wood just outside the opening of their shelter, where the wind would blow the smoke away from them. After pouring the oil over the wood, she tried several matches before a small flame rewarded her efforts.

"You did it," Greg cheered.

Dark black smoke billowed up from the pile of sticks. "I'll have to do this when it's daylight. They should be able to see all this smoke clear back to Kodiak."

She rubbed her hands on her wet pants to try to clean off the oil and dirt. Then she scooted back inside the shelter, where she could watch the fire and be out of the pouring rain. Slowly the flames grew and lit up the night. The rain continued so hard, Lori wondered how the fire could continue to burn without being drowned.

"Keep piling wood around the flames so it will dry out from the fire inside. That and it will keep some of the rain from falling on the flames."

Lori struggled to follow Greg's instructions. "If you'd been around to teach me, I would have been a better Girl Scout."

"You've got it going now. Come inside and rest."

Once more, Lori crawled inside and sat down. She pulled off her raincoat and rain pants and folded them by the door. "Feels better not to have those soggy things on."

"Here." Greg handed her a silver package. "Unfold that and wrap it around you. Supposed to conserve your body heat."

"I feel like I'm wrapped in aluminum foil. Sure you don't plan to barbecue me?" She tried to sound light, but exhaustion and fear invaded her voice.

He reached out to touch her arm. "You've done a fantastic job. Your efforts will save us."

She swallowed hard and said nothing. She knew it would take more than a makeshift shelter and a smoky fire to save them. Trying to think of something else, she turned to her pack. "Maybe I have some more socks in here," she muttered. "Hey, look what I found." She pulled out the three chocolate bars she'd bought for the O'Brien children. "Time for supper."

"What's that?" Greg raised up to see what she held.

"Candy I bought for the kids. Shall we split a bar tonight?"

"You need the energy. You eat it."

"Oh, don't be a martyr. You need your strength, too." She looked at the imprint as she broke the block of chocolate in half and handed him a piece. "We are feasting on eagle tonight."

"Sounds illegal to me, but I'm hungry enough to eat it anyway." He took a bite. "You have any more surprises in that pack?"

She pulled out a pair of jeans and rolled them. "Here, this will make you a pillow." She saved her flannel nightgown to make a pillow for herself. Pushing the pack to the back of the shelter, she tried to curl up on her side. "Not too bad. Maybe tomorrow I can dig out some of the rocks under here."

They lay in silence, listening to the rain pound on the plastic over their head and the wind that tried to rip that plastic from the ropes that held it. "You hurt a lot?" she asked Greg.

"Not so bad if I don't move. Can you see how swollen my leg is?"

She sat up to examine him. She turned the flashlight on to get a better look and promptly turned it off. The swollen, angry flesh told her what pain he must feel. "I hope they come for us first thing in the morning."

"Lori," he said softly, "this storm could last for days."

eleven

The night went on forever. Lori would doze off only to be rudely awakened by a gust of wind that tore at their shelter. She fed more wood into the fire. The light it offered brought more comfort than the meager heat it generated. Greg seemed restless and sometimes groaned with pain. Once or twice she tried to fix the sweater under his broken leg to make him more comfortable.

"Do you think the dawn will ever come?" she asked him.

"Don't they say that it is darkest before the dawn?"

"I think the wind is letting up."

"The rain sure isn't," he answered as the noise on their makeshift roof increased.

Lori tried to sit up and found the side of the tent had formed a pocket that filled with rain. She pushed against it and heard the water cascade off. "I hope that doesn't run back inside here."

"I think you have the floor fixed to keep it out." Greg lay next to the straight side of the tarp that she had tied directly down from the rope. "How is the wood holding up?"

"I only put one piece on at a time. Have a few more to go before we run out." She poked at the feeble flames. "Works good to pile it tepee fashion like you told me. Seems to dry and finally burn. Are you cold?"

"Not too bad. This suit is supposed to keep me from getting hypothermia. How about you?"

"Priscilla may have saved my life with this down jacket."

"Be sure to keep it dry. Down is no good when it gets wet."

"Tell that to the ducks."

Greg's laugh sounded reassuring. "Ducks have oil to keep their feathers dry."

"I used the oil to start a fire. Guess that means I have to use rain gear." She looked out their door. "I think it is getting brighter. Maybe I better get into that rain gear and go gather more wood."

"Do we have any more water?"

"I put the cup and thermos out to gather rain. After last night, they should both be full." Struggling with her soggy rain pants and coat, she finally made her way to where she had wedged the thermos in the rocks. "Oh no!" The cup stood full of water, but the thermos had blown over and tumbled down the rocks to the beach. She retrieved the thermos, putting it beside the tent. The cup she offered to Greg. "Fresh water for breakfast. Cost you a fortune in a fancy restaurant."

Since he didn't know the thermos stood empty, he gulped down the water. "Breakfast may be a little low on calories, but the service is great. Thanks."

Lori put the cup back where it would gather rain and went to look for wood. Fog hindered her search. Trying to ignore her growling stomach, she foraged farther and farther from camp, always keeping the surf to her left. *Don't you dare go into the woods,* she told herself. *In this fog I'd get turned around and lost for sure.* She started a pile of wood on the beach by the boat, and when it got big enough, she would start carrying it piece by piece back to camp.

On her third trip, she checked the cup to find a swallow of water to quench her thirst. "I need to find water."

Crawling back inside to check on Greg, she asked, "Are there bears around here?"

He tried to raise up on one elbow. "No. Bears have more sense than to be out in this weather. They probably have a nice warm, cozy den someplace."

"I hope you're right," she muttered, knowing she would have to explore farther and farther down the beach to keep them in wood and find water.

Greg tried to sit up. "Lying down all the time is killing my back. Wish I could get out and help you."

"So do I, but in the meantime let's see if we can make you more comfortable." Lori pulled her pack from the back corner.

"Could you lean against this?"

He moved his injured leg slowly as he tried to maneuver to where Lori could put the pack behind him. "You have books in here?" he asked, leaning back.

"My Bible," she exclaimed. "Here, I'll take it out." She rearranged the pack with the rolled-up jeans to make a back-rest for him. Her Bible lay on the floor next to Greg.

"Much better," he told her. "You make a good nurse."

"Nursing is not my thing." She poked the struggling fire and piled more wood around the flame to dry. "It's light enough now so I can explore our island some more. Will you be okay?"

"What's the weather like?"

She swallowed hard but knew she had to be honest. "Not good. The wind is down, but the fog is thick."

"No clearance for search helicopters?"

Lori shook her head. "Not yet. Maybe this afternoon it will clear up." A burst of rain hit the tarp over their heads. Both of them looked up without speaking.

"I need to find a fresh water source, so I may be gone for a while."

"Didn't you catch rainwater?"

"The thermos didn't get much and the cup fills slowly." She listened to the pounding rain. "Maybe I should just let it collect on the tarp and drain it from there."

"Might work."

"I'm off." She crawled back out the door. It felt good to stand up after being in the cramped quarters. She said a prayer for Greg, knowing how uncomfortable he must be on the rough ground and not being able to move. "We'll have more chocolate when I get back." Her stomach rumbled at the thought of food.

The fog did not lift. It seemed to shroud everything in eerie white mist. "I should drop bread crumbs," she said aloud, as she tried to keep her bearing and not get lost. *If you had bread, you'd eat it,* her hungry body told her.

She must have walked a mile down the beach before she

came to a stream. She drank her fill, washed her face in the frigid water, and filled the thermos. Going back the way she'd come, she dragged dead branches of trees behind her. Her arms ached, her head felt light, and she stumbled for the umpteenth time.

"I can do it!" she shouted. "Lord, hear my prayer. With Your help I can do it." Singing psalms of praise, she made her way up the beach.

Greg had pulled himself to the door of their shelter. He looked terrified when she came up from the boat. "Are you all right?" he asked, his face white.

"Sure, why?"

"I heard you yelling and I thought something had happened and I couldn't get to you."

"I was singing," she said quietly.

"Singing! You scared me half to death." He sat blocking her way into the shelter.

"I knew my voice didn't sound good, but I didn't think it was that bad," she protested. Secretly, she felt pleased to find he had been worried about her.

Why not? Who would take care of him if you weren't here?

She pushed the unholy thoughts back and knelt by the stack of wood. "Do you have your knife?" She pulled the large branches closer to the fire.

"Maybe I could do that," Greg offered, trying to pull himself farther out the door.

Lori could see the agony every move caused him. "Here. Let me bring this branch to you. Maybe you can just break the limbs up." Instinctively, she knew the inactivity would hurt him more than pulling some branches apart. "I'll go get some more." She pulled the thermos out of her pocket and set it by the tent. "We'll have some water when I get back."

Greg had the branches in his hands, trying to break the limbs off.

Lori made her way back to where she'd found the fallen tree and pulled more branches loose. When she paused to catch her breath, she looked out over the water. The low tide left the surf farther out, and it did not crash as it had yesterday. With the wind down and the waves abating, the stillness took over. "In quietness and confidence shall be my strength," she told the elements. Then, squaring her shoulders one more time, she grabbed the branches and pulled them back to where Greg waited.

He had managed to stoke the fire before dragging himself back inside the shelter to lie back against the pack. Lori found him reading her Bible.

Lori dropped her burden and crawled inside to catch her breath. She didn't say anything when he put the book down. "I brought the thermos in. Do you want some water?"

"You drink first. As hard as you've worked, you need the body fluids."

"With all the rain, I must have absorbed enough fluid to last a month." Lori drank a cup of water and then poured one for Greg. "When you're finished, I'll put the cup out to collect rain again."

"How far did you go to find a stream?"

"Must have been about a mile down and two miles back." Lori lay back on the rough floor of the tent and sighed.

"You better take it easy and conserve your strength."

"It's not clearing." Her voice showed no emotion.

"We'll be here another night." Stress echoed through his voice.

Lori sat up. "Let's have some candy." She tried to sound cheerful. "You'll have to lean forward a minute." She reached for the pack and extracted the chocolate. She helped Greg settle back and put the sweater under his injured leg. "Comfortable?"

"Yes, Nurse Nightingale."

"Well, this time we are having deer," she said, breaking the candy bar in half.

"Eat it slow so your stomach doesn't rebel."

They sat lost in their own thoughts as they sucked on the chocolate, making it last as long as they could.

"I found the Psalms to read," Greg said softly.

"That's what I was singing when you thought I screamed for help."

"You were asking for help, but not from me."

"That's right," she said thoughtfully.

"Have you always been a believer?"

"I grew up in a Christian family. We usually went to church, Sunday school, stuff like that." She paused, then looked up to face him. "I was thirteen when I gave my life to Christ."

"What changed?"

She shrugged. "I don't know that there ever was a big change. Life went on the same way, but then I knew the Lord was in control."

"Even when your parents died?"

Lori sighed. "When my parents were killed, I screamed at God. How dare He take my wonderful father and mother away from me. My life had a pattern, and all that changed on one icy patch of road."

"God broke the pattern."

"Not really," she said thoughtfully. "We have free choice, you know. The Lord isn't some kind of puppeteer pulling our strings. It took awhile, but finally I realized God didn't make my parents go to a teachers' meeting and He didn't make their car slide off the road." She patted the Bible that lay between them. "He did say He would comfort me in my grief. And He promised that somehow all things work together for good when we commit our lives into God's hands."

"So it was your father's fault for hitting the ice."

"He didn't want to die, if that's what you mean. I know he didn't want to hurt my mother. He loved her very much." She looked at Greg, trying to read his thoughts. "Life is new each day. If we try to live that life to the glory of God, we find happiness, and when we find sorrow and grief, we have the strength to bear it and learn from it. End of sermon." She got back on her hands and knees to crawl to the door and check the fire.

"I'd like to hear more."

"Really? I don't want to bore you."

"I admire you, Lori. Watching you these past weeks has taught me that you have something I would like to have. Maybe it's faith."

"I'm not much of a Bible pounder. I like to read the Word and try to figure out what it means. Mostly I want to live what it means."

"You do. You certainly do," he said with quiet conviction.

She grinned. "You don't have to butter me up to get the other chocolate bar. I'll share."

"That's what I mean. You're always willing to share." He tried to move his back against the pack. "Kalissa's people are like that. Always wanting to give gifts and share."

"Oh, Greg, my presents are in the boat."

"What?"

"My presents. Every child in the village had made something for me." She pulled the now dirty wool cap off her head. "One of the senior girls knit this for me." She put the cap down. "Rika and I packed everything in a box and wrapped it in two plastic bags. Do you think they will be okay?"

"Did they give you any food?"

"Oh, Greg. Stop thinking about food."

"Aren't you hungry?"

"My tummy stopped speaking in anything but growls yesterday. You want some more water?"

"Yes, I suppose so."

The light grew dim as the early dusk fell around them. They took turns sipping water before Lori put the cup back out to catch more rain. "Not raining right now. Maybe the fog will lift in the morning."

"I hope so," Greg sighed. His swollen leg lay on the folded sweater. The zipper at the bottom of the coverall was fully open. Lori had cut both the boot and sock off and tried to wrap his foot in a shirt from her pack.

"Is your foot cold? Maybe I should try putting more clothes over it."

"I don't think I can stand anything on it. Besides that, what little bit is left in your pack makes a pillow for me."

"The boat cushions are soaked, but if I put a couple inside the pack, the wet wouldn't soak through. I'll go find them and see if we can make you more comfortable."

Getting up quickly made her head spin. She shook off the dizzy spell and made her way to the boat. *Why didn't I think of this before?* she scolded herself. *Guess I didn't expect to be stuck here so long,* she admitted. Using the flashlight, she dug out two cushions and made her way back to the shelter. "Is that better?" she asked, putting the now full pack behind Greg.

"Much." He wiggled his shoulders back against the cushions. "How about you? Can you find a comfortable spot?"

By this time, she was out of her rain gear and sat with the silver survival blanket wrapped around here. "I'm okay," she said, as much to convince herself as to reassure him. Secretly, she felt like the dampness had moved into her bones permanently. Her feet were the worst. Without wool socks, her toes felt like ice all the time. She had pulled on three pairs of cotton anklets and made sure to keep her feet dry, but still the cold penetrated to the core. "Just tired," she told Greg.

"You must be, hauling wood and water and waiting on me."

"Can you sleep or does the pain keep you awake?"

"I try not to think about it. Are you tired? You want me to keep quiet so you can sleep?"

"Sleep! What is it, about seven o'clock at night?"

Greg held his watch toward the firelight. "It's six-thirty."

"Time for Marmalade's warm milk. Who will take care of him until we get back?"

"Scott knows where the food is. Marmalade doesn't much like the boy, but he'll eat the food Scott puts out. Never have figured out why that cat took to you. He's never been friends with anyone."

"Where did you get him?"

"Rika found him living in the woodpile as a tiny kitten. She thought I needed company and gave him to me."

"How did you get him home?"

"Put him in a cardboard box. He and I had a smooth trip in the boat that day." He chuckled. "Good thing. He'd never have been able to take care of me like you have."

"I had a wonderful visit with Rika and Kalissa. Will you fly Rika to Monk's so she can visit my school?"

"If we ever get out of here." The strain of their situation sounded in his tone.

Lori fought back her own fatigue. *I've got to keep him thinking positive,* she thought. "Kalissa told me about her husband. Sad story. I wonder why she never remarried?"

"We never could find out much about her life after she left the Aleutians until she settled in Kodiak."

"Wouldn't she talk about it?"

"Kalissa didn't want to talk about anything before she took us kids to raise. She would tell us her life ended when Kot-le-wah left and started again when she found us."

"Do you know how long she'd lived with your parents?"

"A couple years, I think. I hardly ever remember a time when she wasn't there."

"It must have been very hard on you losing your mother and father so young."

"Without Kalissa I don't know what I would have done."

"Gone to live with Olga."

"Rika's been blabbing. She told you how Olga came looking for me?"

"Yes. She also told me Olga is your aunt."

"True. She did try to find me, and I don't know why the authorities didn't help her more. Guess it didn't help that Kalissa couldn't read, and if letters came, she didn't understand what was in them."

"It's turned out okay."

"Is that your Lord making good out of a bad situation?"

"It happened—if you only believe."

"Well, I didn't believe and it still happened."

"Maybe Olga did."

"Never thought of that. She did set me up with the preacher to live with. Even if that did turn out bad."

"No it didn't. You were there to help those folks stay in their own home a little while longer."

"You sound like Pollyanna."

"Sorry, didn't mean to." She fed some branches into the fire and listened to the crackle. She tried to change the subject by telling him about the party the children had planned for her at the village. "All that food. There I go thinking about my stomach again."

"Maybe you can patent a new kind of diet."

She giggled. "Bet Sandy will be the first to sign up. She told me she gained fifteen pounds the first couple of months at Monk's."

The night dragged on. Lori fell asleep curled in a ball with the silver blanket hugged around her. The exhaustion of work, worry, and lack of food caught up with her. Even on the uneven ground, she slept long and hard. The rain ceased, and without it pounding on the tarp, there was no sound to wake her.

Coming awake at last, she stretched her cramped muscles and looked around. No light broke the darkness. "The fire," she gasped. "I've let the fire go out."

"What's wrong?" Greg muttered from his side of the tent.

"The fire is out. Do we have any matches left?"

"I put them in my pocket."

She heard him moving. She unwrapped the blanket and felt around for her boots and rain gear.

"Can you find the flashlight?" he asked.

"It's here someplace." She tried patting the ground near the door. "Found it," she cried, clicking the light on.

Greg put one hand over his eyes while holding out his other hand with the matches. "Did you get some gasoline?"

"No. I'll have to try to collect some in the old oilcan."

"Unhook the tube from the motor and pump that rubber ball in the line. That's what I use to prime the motor."

"I'll try." Lori took the flashlight and crawled out of the shelter. First she had to find the oilcan, then she started for the boat. The sky in the east held the promise of a new day as she found the line and followed Greg's instruction. With the can of gasoline in one hand and the flashlight in the other, she carefully made her way back to the tent.

"I can hold the light if that will help."

She handed him the flashlight. "I got the gasoline. Now I'll pile up the wood like you taught me."

"Once you pour the gas on, stand back when you throw the match. It will explode."

"Is the tarp in danger?"

"How much gasoline do you plan to use?"

"Is a cupful enough?" she asked timidly.

"Won't know until we try."

Within moments, she had a cheerful blaze going. Rubbing her hands on her wet pants, she tried to get rid of the gasoline smell. "I'll go get us some water. The cup and thermos should be full." Struggling in the dim light of the predawn, she found the thermos propped up in the rocks. The cup stood partially full, but the thermos felt empty. Everything dripped. The ground under her feet felt like a sponge, but no rain fell. She took what water they had back to camp and shared it with Greg.

"Maybe there will be more collected in the tarp," she said, looking to see how much of a bulge had formed in the roof. "When it gets light, I'll go back to the stream."

"We need to get the flare gun ready."

"Flare gun?"

"In the boat I have flares we can set off when we hear a plane or helicopter. That way they will spot us."

"Weren't they in the survival pack?"

"No. I have the gun and flares in an orange pack. It should be under the console with my tools."

"I've never fired a gun in my life."

"You find it and bring it here. I'll have it all set so you only have to point at the sky and pull the trigger."

"Right now I can't see the sky," she moaned.

"Isn't it getting light?"

Realizing too late what she had admitted, Lori looked stricken. "Greg, if anything, the fog is worse."

"It will clear with daylight."

"I pray you're right." She poked the fire and shoved back the knowledge she would have to start finding more wood to last the day. The small pieces she was strong enough to carry didn't last long. "I'll go look for the flare gun." She struggled to her feet once again and headed for the boat. *Was it farther away or did it just seem that way?* she wondered, as she dragged her feet down to the beach again.

The hours went by like days. The fog lay thick in the trees and out over the water. The wind did not stir and the rain did not fall. Fog masked every movement. She did not even see a bird in flight. How could she? They would have to have been only a few feet off the water to still be visible.

"I'm going for water now," she told Greg.

"Be careful."

Even their words seemed cloaked in mist and gloom. Slowly putting one foot in front of the other, Lori made her way back to the stream and filled the thermos. The two scant cups of water she'd gotten off the tarp were gone. This would have to last them the rest of the day. "I can't make it this far again," she moaned. She searched for wood and tried to drag more from the fallen tree she'd found a half mile from camp.

Greg lay on his back, the pack pushed aside. "Are you asleep?" she whispered when she got back.

"No." His voice was barely audible.

How much more of this could he stand? "We still have one chocolate bar. Can you eat some?"

"Only a bite. Save the rest for later."

"This time we have a bear." She tried to be cheerful, but her own discouragement became harder and harder to overcome. "Greg, how long can we last?"

"Till spring." He tried to sit up, and she saw the agony that sent him down flat on his back.

She put the bite of candy in his mouth and put a similar piece in her own mouth. Stomach cramps twisted her body double. She curled up without taking off her rain clothes.

Sharing stories took too much effort. Both of them dozed off and on between sips of water and trying to keep the fire burning. As darkness started to push away the short day, Lori made one more trip to find wood. "I think we have enough for the night. Will you wake me up if I don't have enough wood on the fire?"

Greg answered with a sigh. "Why do we need a fire?"

"I don't know. I guess I like the light it gives us." She put her hands toward the flames. "And it is warmer with one going."

"Yes, I'll wake you."

She looked closely at him. Was he drifting in and out of consciousness? She tried to fix the cushions inside the pack to make him more comfortable. "What can I do for you?"

"Pray for me," he whispered.

He must be delirious, she thought, and then scolded herself for the unkind thought. "Yes, Greg, I will pray without ceasing."

The night wore on. Darkness did not even hide the fog. She could see the flames reflect off the mist that moved silently around them. "How long, Lord? How long?" she said aloud.

She pulled off the heavy, wet rain clothes and curled up with the survival blanket. She lay staring at the fire, thinking of home. What would Fred say if he could see her now? Definitely not bank president wife material. Willing herself to wake often and feed the fire, she dozed off. She didn't keep count of the number of times she pushed more wood toward the flames to dry and eventually burn. The night refused to end.

Greg seemed restless, tossing his head and arms about. The rest of his body lay still. His leg looked grotesque in the firelight where the swelling and red angry flesh lay uncovered. He couldn't even stand the light shirt she tried to keep over his foot. He lay with the foot toward the fire, so some heat reached him.

Lori sat up. Her head felt light and dizzy. Her stomach cramped and her muscles protested all the wood she'd hauled. With a prayer for strength, she crawled toward the door to pull more wood to the fire. She could see the beach in the light streaking the eastern sky. "I can see the beach," she cried.

"Huh, what?" Greg stirred.

Turning back to him, she repeated, "Greg, I can see the beach. The fog is lifting." She crawled outside, forgetting to put her boots on and soaking her socks. "Praise the Lord, the fog is lifting."

"Lori, get in here and put your boots on. We aren't saved yet. They still have to find us."

"Do you have the flare gun ready?"

"Lori, it isn't light yet. Don't get your hopes too high. It may take awhile to find us."

Sighing, she knew Greg was right. But as the light grew, so did her hopes. Recklessly she piled the fire high, not trying to conserve what wood she had left. "I better go for water again."

"Do you think you can make it?" he asked.

Trying to mask her weakness, she nodded her head. "Like you say, it may be awhile and we should at least have water."

The mile to the stream seemed to grow each time she made the trek. Her head ached and her boots seemed to weigh five pounds each. The wet socks added to her discomfort. Coming back to the camp, she sat down with a thump on the floor of their shelter. By now the tarp inside was tracked with mud and bits of bark and leaves. "I'm a lousy housekeeper," she said, picking up some of the litter.

"I promise to vacuum for you later today," he said with a weak smile.

Looking at his drawn, white face, she knew what the humor cost him. "How about a drink first?"

"You buying?"

"Only the first round."

As she held the cup out to him, she heard a faint buzzing. Still holding her hand out, she stopped to listen. "Do you hear it?"

He nodded his head.

She pulled on her boots, grabbed the flare gun, and ran for the beach. Holding the gun in both hands, she aimed toward the speck in the sky, closed her eyes, and pulled the trigger.

twelve

Lori fell to her knees, offering silent prayers of thanks until she heard the helicopter overhead. Standing, she waved to the aircraft from the rocky shore. She moved back as the chopper descended. As soon as they were on land, the door popped open and a man ran to her.

"Please help Greg," she begged, pointing to the blue tarp shelter. "He's got a broken leg."

As a second Coast Guardsman approached, the one by Lori shouted, "Got a man hurt. Better check him out." He then turned to Lori. "Your friend will be cared for, miss. Now let's get you into the chopper and comfortable."

"I'm all right. Just tired, dirty, and hungry." She didn't object to being led to the waiting craft after she saw men carrying medical bags and a crash board toward the shelter. The young man got her seated and brought her a cup of warm broth.

"Sip it slow. Give your stomach time to adjust to food again," he advised her.

Lori cradled the cup in her hands. She looked at her broken nails and grimy fingers. "Warm water and a bath," she said. "All I need is to be clean again."

The medic checking her laughed. "You'll soon have that. Right now I want to check your vital signs. Can you get out of that heavy coat?"

Lori pulled off the rain gear and down jacket. They lay in a dirty pile on the floor. She felt like she'd shed a huge weight at the same time as she'd taken off the coats. As the burden of responsibility for their survival fell away, a feeling of lethargy took its place. "I'm going home and sleep for a week," she murmured.

"Are you okay now?"

She nodded and sipped more broth.

"I'm going to help my buddies get your friend aboard. Will you be all right?"

"Yes, please help Greg," she repeated.

When the crash board with Greg strapped in was loaded aboard, Lori tried to go to his side.

"We gave him a shot of pain medication. He's pretty well out of it."

She backed away as an IV bottle was attached and the medics worked over Greg. "Is he all right?" she inquired.

One of the men turned to her. "Worried about you until we put him under. Said you'd taken care of him since Sunday." He smiled encouragingly. "You did a good job."

The trip to Kodiak seemed to take only minutes. Time had lost meaning for Lori. She sat back and let others take over. She watched Greg, who appeared to sleep comfortably for the first time since the accident.

"You stay here while we get Greg into the ambulance," one medic told her.

Dutifully, she waited. The flashing lights through the window told her Greg would soon be in a hospital. She looked up when a Coast Guardsman approached her. "Would you like to ride in the ambulance with your friend?"

"Yes, please." She unstrapped her seat belt and followed him out of the chopper.

"You may be able to give them some more information," he added.

At the hospital, nurses took charge of getting Greg admitted and assured Lori doctors would be checking him out promptly. "We also want to check you over."

"I'm fine. Just dirty and tired. All I want is a bath and a place to sleep. Can someone take me to a motel?"

"Still need to look you over. You've been through quite an ordeal."

Lori let herself be questioned and her vital signs checked again. It seemed hours before she finally heard the doctor say, "You won't have to be admitted if you have a place to stay."

"She does. She's going home with me," a woman said. Lori turned toward the voice. "Hi, I'm Tom's wife, Nancy. He called me from the airport and told me to come fetch you as soon as you were released."

"Hal's helper?"

"Hey, you're doing great to remember that. Come on now, let's get out of this place."

Gratefully, Lori followed this newfound friend.

Nancy chattered as she led Lori to the parking lot. "Joe's out on the Coast Guard cutter. They got a distress call in the Shelikof Straight, so he'll be gone a few days. We'll take you to his place." She opened the door of a car and watched Lori buckle herself in. "We only have a one-bedroom place, but we're right next door, so you won't really be alone."

"All I want is a long, hot shower and a place to sleep," Lori moaned. "I've never felt so tired."

"Doc said it's from not eating and probably the relief of being rescued." She patted her pregnant tummy. "After Junior arrives, I'll probably have to go on a crash diet, too."

Lori looked out the window, seeing nothing and barely listening to Nancy while they traveled to Joe's trailer. "Doesn't he keep his house locked?" Lori asked.

"He leaves a key with us in case someone needs a place to stay. All part of the service our Bible study group tries to provide. Lots of people get stranded in this country."

"Thank you" were the only words Lori could think to say.

She followed Nancy into the trailer where she'd laughed and talked with Joe and his friends a week before. It seemed more like a month. Looking down at her filthy jeans, she chose to sit in a kitchen chair.

"I'll be right back. I only live next door and I'll find something you can put on."

Lori nodded, too lethargic to think straight.

Nancy bounced back through the door a short time later, carrying pajamas and a robe. "Why don't you get that shower you want and wrap up in this bathrobe. Leave your dirty clothes in the bathroom."

"We can bury them later," Lori tried to joke, looking at the smudges on her wool sweater. She made her way to the bathroom and stripped off the offending, smelly, dirty clothes she'd put on last Sunday in Rika's bedroom. Unbinding her braided hair felt wonderful. Standing in the warm water with soap suds flowing over her felt like heaven. She let the water cascade through her hair and thanked God for the gift of being clean and warm. Half an hour later, dressed in the pajamas and robe Nancy provided, Lori went back toward the living room. Wonderful smells greeted her.

"I fixed some soup. I know you have to get used to food slowly and thought that might taste good."

"Smells fantastic. Makes my mouth water." Lori sat at the kitchen table and savored the warm bowl of broth and vegetables. She sat back, stretched, and said, "All I want now is to sleep for a week."

"Come on, I'll show you your room. I put an extra blanket on the bottom of the bed in case you get cold."

Lori breathed one last prayer of thanks before falling into a deep, refreshing sleep.

❧

She woke to the smell of coffee brewing. Looking at the clock, she sat up with a start. "I slept fourteen hours!"

"You sure did," Nancy said from the doorway. "I was beginning to think you'd beat Rip Van Winkle."

Lori swung her legs out of the blankets and pulled the robe back around her. "That coffee smells delicious."

"I brought your clothes back. The sweater can't go in the dryer, so it isn't dry. I brought you one of my sweatshirts to put on instead." Nancy lay the clean clothes on the foot of the bed. "Get dressed and I'll go fix you some toast."

Lori looked in wonder at her fresh, clean underwear and jeans. "You washed all this for me?"

"Didn't think you'd want to wear that bathrobe to go home," Nancy quipped.

"How can I ever thank you enough? You don't even know me and you're waiting on me like this."

"We're sisters in Christ," Nancy said quietly. "Now get dressed and come eat some breakfast."

With food in her stomach, clean hair, clean body, and clean clothes, Lori felt fantastic. Sitting back from the table cradling another cup of coffee, she asked, "Do you think we could go see Greg?"

"Let's call the hospital to see if he can have visitors. Yesterday they were talking about surgery and, I don't know when they planned to do it." Nancy went to the phone while Lori sipped on her coffee.

Nancy put the phone down. "Won't be able to see him for a while. He's being airlifted to Seattle."

Lori sat up with a start. "What?"

"They're flying him down to Seattle to one of the big hospitals there. Seems it's a bad break and, not getting it set right away, they want to make sure he gets the best possible care."

"His leg looked awful, but I thought it was because it got so swollen. Maybe I should have tried to put a splint on it."

"I'm sure you did fine. It's just we are a small town with a small hospital. Lots of people go south for medical care. We even thought about me having the baby in Seattle."

Somewhat mollified, Lori looked down. "I don't have any shoes," she yelped.

"Why don't we go shopping?"

"I don't have any money."

"Not to worry. You tell the shop owner why and he'll be glad to extend you credit."

"The Alaskan way. Will I ever get used to it?"

Lori scuffed her way into the store in Nancy's slippers and purchased not only some shoes but some underthings and a sweatshirt of her own to wear until she could fly home. "Can't expect you to keep doing my laundry while I sleep," she told Nancy. "Now I need to go buy some candy bars."

"Candy bars!"

Lori explained how she had purchased the candy for some of her students and it had wound up being the only food they'd had for three days. Lori bought not only the candy bars for Peggy, Mark, and Aaron, she bought candy kisses for all her students.

When Tom came home Thursday night, he told Lori that Hal planned to fly out to Monk's Island the next day.

"I'm going home," she sighed.

The weather dawned clear on Friday. Lori called the airport and made arrangements to be on the plane to Monk's. It seemed natural to climb into the copilot's seat and look out over the water, islands, and timber below as they flew toward her home.

"You and Greg were right about there." Hall pointed to a group of islands in Marmont Bay.

"Never did ask how they found us," she said.

"Oh, we looked over the maps, figured in the currents and the wind direction. Knowing when and where you started out helped."

"You were in on the rescue, too?"

"When someone is lost, everyone helps until they're found."

"Like the one lost sheep."

Hal smiled. "You could say that, yes."

When Lori stepped off the plane on the beach of Monk's Island, she stared in wonder. "Nikita!"

"Hi, Lori. Are you okay now?"

"Why are you here?"

"My dad and I got coordinates from the Coast Guard and found Greg's boat. We towed it to the village yesterday, got the motors working fine, and I brought it back here today. Oh, your things are in your wanagan."

"Wow! I can't believe how everyone has taken care of us." She put her hands up. "I know, I know, it's the Alaskan way."

Nikita laughed. "I'm going to catch a ride back to the village with Hal. How's Greg?"

"They took him to Seattle. I haven't heard any more. I gave them Rika's name and address as next of kin. I thought she could handle the authorities better than Kalissa if they need information."

"She handles all of us. Taking care of her brother will be a piece of cake for her."

Lori looked down as she felt a tug on her pant legs. Mark stood on one side, Aaron on the other. Peggy stood only a few feet away. "You got lost. Did you come home now?" Aaron asked.

Lori knelt to pull the three children into her embrace. "I'm not lost anymore. I've come home to stay."

"Rika will be glad to know you're all right. We'll see you soon," Nikita told her as he boarded the plane.

Lori waved good-bye to Nikita, then let the children lead her to their home. Word spread fast and by the time they reached the O'Briens' mobile home, a crowd waited to greet her. Many cries of joy and hugs of loving welcome awaited her.

"Your prayers kept us safe," Lori told her friends as she recounted the story of their survival.

"How much weight did you lose?" Sandy demanded.

"Don't try it, Sandy. Steve will love you more with a few extra pounds rather than a vacation in a wet, cold tarp with no food."

"Hawaii does sound better," she admitted.

Still tired and a little weak from her ordeal, Lori begged to be allowed to go home after a couple hours of celebration. Walking up to her trailer, she looked at the sky and thought again of the fog and gloom of the days in their makeshift shelter. "Thank You, Lord, even for the rain."

As she approached her back steps, a familiar shape appeared out of the dark. "Marmalade!" She stooped down to pet her furry friend. He rubbed and purred and could not seem to get enough loving. "You've been alone a long time, old friend. Come in and we'll see if I can't fix you some warm milk."

She opened the door and turned on the light to see the box she and Rika had packed so carefully. Her waterproof pack sat next to it. She thought of Greg trying to use it to lean on and hoped he was more comfortable in the hospital in Seattle. "Must be getting good care," she said, giving Marmalade another pat before picking up the box and taking it to her kitchen. She put milk to warm and sorted through her treasures from the children in Uzinkie.

At the bottom of the box, she found a package she didn't remember packing. Unwrapping it, she found the picture Rika had painted of the anemones. Tears filled her eyes. The note with it said, If my brother weren't so pigheaded, we could be sisters, too. Lori sighed and went to fix the cat a bowl of milk and herself a cup of cocoa.

Marmalade stayed close to her as she put things away. Whenever she stopped long enough, he rubbed against her legs or stood on his hind legs and pushed against her hand. Tired from the excitement of the day, Lori went to bed early, with the big tabby cat curled as close to her as he could get.

Liz and Betty had kept the school going. Lori used the weekend to go over papers and prepare lesson plans for the next week. She also took time to read her mail again.

The weekly envelope from Priscilla had been extra thick. Lori picked up the pages written in Bob's hand and read them again.

> *You must be psychic. The day your letter came*
> *suggesting we make a nursery out of your bedroom,*
> *the doctor confirmed you are going to be an aunt.*

Tears of joy filled her eyes as she read and reread both letters. The excitement and anticipation her brother and his wife expressed made her finally admit Bob had found a perfect wife. Her brother had found happiness in spite of her selfish wishes to keep him for herself. *Maybe I just grew up,* she said in her mind.

Writing to Bob and Priscilla, she told them:

> *I feel like I left home yesterday and I've been gone*
> *forever.*

She didn't tell them about being lost for days and surviving in the Alaskan wilderness. *They wouldn't understand,* she told herself. You have to see it and live in this country to believe it, Lori wrote. She gave up trying to describe how she felt. She sent pictures of the beauty of the land and pictures and stories of her students.

> *I'll come back to visit my nephew or niece next summer, but this is my land. The great land where I want to stay.*

The letter to Fred was harder to compose. Trying to imagine life with Fred made her giggle. She could only write how much she felt honored by his proposal, but she didn't feel worthy to be his wife. *Worthy! I'd be bored to tears. No bears, no shipwrecks, no fog and rain that goes on for days. What a way to live.* She smiled, sealing the letter and licking the stamp. "No, I'd never make it as a bank president's wife," she told the cat sitting on the desk beside her. "You've convinced me to be an old maid and raise cats." Marmalade purred in response.

Life fell back into routine. There were school lessons and coffee klatches with the women on the dark afternoons after school. Her little friends came often for stories and cookies. No one heard from Greg. She'd found her Bible in the pack. It had some bent and dirty pages as a reminder of the days waiting for rescue. She wondered if anything Greg had read helped him get through the days of pain while she scavenged for wood and water.

Time passed quickly. Talk and plans were being made for Thanksgiving. The huge potluck of all the people on Monk's would be the order of the day.

The cranberry juice entrusted to Lori stayed frozen in her freezer. She had the punch recipe and had ordered the rest of the ingredients.

Thanksgiving would also be a farewell for Sandy and Steve as well as a few other single men from the bunkhouse.

"Wonder if Greg will be back?" Theresa asked.

"I don't know," Lori said. "I guess we could contact his office to see. I kind of expected he would write to one of us."

"If he doesn't come home soon, Marmalade won't know him. The kids say that cat lies on the davenport right next to you while you read to them." She laughed. "He'll even put up with kids to be close to you."

"He's a lot of company," Lori admitted aloud. Inwardly she wondered for the umpteenth time why she had heard nothing from Greg. Was his injury worse than they thought, or did he just not want to contact her?

An evening just a few days before Thanksgiving, Lori read, listened to the radio, and petted Marmalade, who lay next to her. A thump brought both of them alert. The cat jumped down at the second thump, his fur raised on his back. Lori ran to her back door to see what caused the noise.

Greg stood on crutches on the top step trying to open the door and hold a plastic grocery bag at the same time.

"Welcome home," cried Lori. "Come in. When did you get back?"

"I flew in with Hal and the turkeys." He worked his way down the hall to the living room. "Hello, cat. Do you remember me?" Greg dropped into the chair, laying his crutches and bag on the floor at his side. Marmalade sniffed his cast and eyed his master for a moment before deciding it would be safe to jump on him.

Lori followed Greg as far as the kitchen, where she stopped to put the tea kettle to heat. "Tell me about Seattle. What did they do to your leg?"

"Seems I'd mashed it up pretty good. Orthopedist broke it where it had started to heal wrong and pinned it back together. Going to take awhile, but I'll heal good as new."

"Were you in the hospital all this time?"

He grinned. "No. I've been visiting Olga and her family."

"Your aunt?" Lori asked in wonder.

"Lying in the tent you built, I had a lot of time to think. Decided it was time to get to know all my family. Didn't expect to do it quite this way, but while I was in the hospital,

I called her. She came everyday to see me, and as soon as I could get out, she took me home. She took me to rehabilitation, doctor appointments, took almost as good care of me as you did."

Lori put the cup of tea where he could reach it and curled up on the davenport. Marmalade promptly curled up next to her.

Greg raised his eyebrows but said nothing. Instead he reached for the bag he'd dropped by the crutches. "I brought you something." He pulled out a box of candy.

Lori laughed. "You and everyone else on this island is determined to get me to gain weight. I really didn't lose that much in three days."

"I just thought if we decide to live on chocolate again, we should have a fancier brand."

"Oh, now you're saying you didn't like my candy bars."

Greg joined in the laughter. "Your brand tasted like ambrosia at the time." He reached for the bag again. "I brought you this, too." He handed her a Bible. "I kind of messed up your other one."

Lori didn't know what to say. She got up and went to take the Bible. The beautiful leather cover was imprinted with her name.

"Olga helped me pick it out."

Lori held the Bible and looked at him. Marmalade sat on the couch waiting for her to come back to pet him. "Olga?" she whispered.

"We spent many hours together. I learned a lot about my parents. About my mother, especially. Olga even has pictures of her that she is having reprinted for me." His voice sounded soft and gentle. "I'm glad I went there. I've filled in a lot of holes in my past. I've gotten to know my parents again." He looked at her. "Can you understand I had to get to know them before I could let them go?"

"I think I understand. Grief is a hard thing to deal with and some of us never do."

"Olga took me to the church where my parents used to attend. I got to know the pastor." He smiled. "Not the one who was there when my parents were, but the one who is there now. He spent many hours with me." Again he looked at her, begging to be understood. "I had a lot of questions."

"Did he answer them?" she asked in a quiet tone.

"Some of them. There are things I will have to figure out for myself." He looked at her Bible. "Olga got me one, too. I have a lot of learning to do."

Puzzled, Lori didn't know what to say.

"Lori, I gave my heart to Christ. Will you help me learn to follow Him?"

Her eyes filled with tears. She sat back on the couch and absently reached for the cat. "I'll try," she offered. The tears fell on Marmalade, who stood up to lick them off her cheeks.

"I'm jealous of that cat."

The anger in his voice brought her up short until she saw his grin.

"Could you ever love me like you love that animal?"

"What are you saying?" she asked, taking her hand off the tabby.

"Well, my cat seems to have a lot more sense than I do. I've loved you ever since you fell off that plane in high heels last summer. It has taken me this long to admit it both to you and myself. Do you think you could find it in your heart to take in a couple of former confirmed bachelors?" He pointed to the cat curled up at her side again. "It appears that Marmalade has already moved in. Can you find room for me, too?"

Lori's mind went blank. She dared not think.

Greg sat forward in his chair, reaching for her. "Lori, will you be my wife, my spiritual partner—" Marmalade jumped off the couch and stretched, and Greg grinned, "And take care of my cat?"

Joy exploded throughout her being. Falling on her knees in front of Greg, she whispered, "Yes, with God's help."

He took her face in his hands and bent to kiss her lips. Marmalade jumped onto the arm of Greg's chair and purred.

A Letter To Our Readers

Dear Reader:

In order that we might better contribute to your reading enjoyment, we would appreciate your taking a few minutes to respond to the following questions. When completed, please return to the following:

Rebecca Germany, Managing Editor
Heartsong Presents
P.O. Box 719
Uhrichsville, Ohio 44683

1. Did you enjoy reading *The Alaskan Way?*
   ❏ Very much. I would like to see more books
      by this author!
   ❏ Moderately
      I would have enjoyed it more if _____

   _____

2. Are you a member of **Heartsong Presents**? ❏Yes ❏No
   If no, where did you purchase this book? _____

   _____

3. What influenced your decision to purchase this
   book? (Check those that apply.)

   ❏ Cover   ❏ Back cover copy

   ❏ Title   ❏ Friends

   ❏ Publicity   ❏ Other_____

4. How would you rate, on a scale from 1 (poor) to 5
   (superior), the cover design? _____

5. On a scale from 1 (poor) to 10 (superior), please rate the following elements.

___Heroine   ___Plot

___Hero   ___Inspirational theme

___Setting   ___Secondary characters

6. What settings would you like to see covered in **Heartsong Presents** books?_____

_____

_____

7. What are some inspirational themes you would like to see treated in future books?_____

_____

_____

8. Would you be interested in reading other **Heartsong Presents** titles?   ❏ Yes   ❏ No

9. Please check your age range:
   ❏ Under 18   ❏ 18-24   ❏ 25-34
   ❏ 35-45   ❏ 46-55   ❏ Over 55

10. How many hours per week do you read? _____

Name _____

Occupation_____

Address_____

City_____ State_____ Zip _____

Heart♥ong

CONTEMPORARY ROMANCE IS CHEAPER BY THE DOZEN!

Any 12 Heartsong Presents **titles** for only $26.95 **

Buy any assortment of twelve Heartsong Presents titles and save 25% off of the already discounted price of $2.95 each!

**plus $1.00 shipping and handling per order and sales tax where applicable.

HEARTSONG PRESENTS *TITLES AVAILABLE NOW:*

(If ordering from this page, please remember to include it with the order form.)

········· Presents ·········

Great Inspirational Romance at a Great Price!

Heartsong Presents books are inspirational romances in contemporary and historical settings, designed to give you an enjoyable, spirit-lifting reading experience. You can choose wonderfully written titles from some of today's best authors like Veda Boyd Jones, Yvonne Lehman, Tracie Peterson, Nancy N. Rue, and many others.

When ordering quantities less than twelve, above titles are $2.95 each.
Not all titles may be available at time of order.

Heartsong Presents
Love Stories Are Rated G!

That's for godly, gratifying, and of course, great! If you love a thrilling love story, but don't appreciate the sordidness of some popular paperback romances, **Heartsong Presents** is for you. In fact, **Heartsong Presents** is the *only inspirational romance book club*, the only one featuring love stories where Christian faith is the primary ingredient in a marriage relationship.

Sign up today to receive your first set of four, never before published Christian romances. Send no money now; you will receive a bill with the first shipment. You may cancel at any time without obligation, and if you aren't completely satisfied with any selection, you may return the books for an immediate refund!

Imagine. . .four new romances every four weeks—two historical, two contemporary—with men and women like you who long to meet the one God has chosen as the love of their lives. . .all for the low price of $9.97 postpaid.

To join, simply complete the coupon below and mail to the address provided. **Heartsong Presents** romances are rated G for another reason: They'll arrive *Godspeed!*